...~hsh~d two years later. Since then she has gone on to write numerous successful novels, including *Thursday's Child*, winner of the 2002 Guardian Children's Fiction Prize; *What the Birds See*, which won the prestigious Age Book of the Year in Australia; *Stripes of the Sidestep Wolf* and *Surrender*, which was a Michael L. Printz Honor Book. *The Ghost's Child* has been shortlisted for the Commonwealth Writers' Prize.

By the same author

Stripes of the Sidestep Wolf

Thursday's Child

What the Birds See

Surrender

The Silver Donkey

The Ghost's Child

Sonya Hartnett

WALKER
BOOKS

Published by arrangement with Penguin Books Australia Ltd

First published in Great Britain 2008 by Walker Books Ltd
87 Vauxhall Walk, London SE11 5HJ

10 9 8 7 6 5 4 3 2 1

This book has been typeset in Bembo

Printed and bound in Great Britain by Clays ltd, St Ives plc

British Library Cataloguing in Publication Data:
a catalogue record for this book is available from the British Library

ISBN 978-1-4063-1319-2

www.walkerbooks.co.uk

FSC
Mixed Sources
Product group from well-managed
forests and other controlled sources
Cert no. SGS - COC - 2061
www.fsc.org
© 1996 Forest Stewardship Council

For Julie Watts

One damp silvery afternoon an old lady came home from walking her dog and found a boy sitting in her lounge room on the floral settee. The boy hadn't been invited, so the old lady was surprised to see him. It wasn't a large boy, and he looked annoyed and bored, as if he had been waiting for her for some time. The lounge room was cold, and the tip of his nose had turned softly pink, which made the old lady feel sorry for him. "You should have lit the fire," she said, and pressed a button and twisted a dial, causing flames to jump up like can-can dancers inside the silver chest of the heater. Her guest didn't answer, but looked more aggrieved: being a boy of a certain age, he had a taste for suffering manfully, and preferred not to be given advice. "Would you like a cup of tea?" she asked him. "I'm about to make a pot."

The boy thought for a moment; then said morosely, "Yes please."

The old lady was relieved to hear that he knew about *please* and *thank you*. At least he had some manners. She hung up her cardigan and went to the kitchen and filled the kettle with water. The kitchen was clean and lined with green cupboards; on the speckled bench were rectangular tins for flour and coffee and rice. On the windowsill was a posy of drooping fuchsias from the garden. Although she couldn't see him, the old lady knew that her curious visitor was still sitting on the settee, hands folded in his lap, waiting and watching for her. She tried not to wonder what he intended to do or say. She determined to keep her thoughts very blank, so she wouldn't race ahead of him or turn a wrong corner in her mind. She couldn't help smiling at the thought of him seated so casually in her lounge room. It was odd, and also somehow flattering, as when a stray cat chooses your house to call home.

While the kettle boiled she busied herself putting biscuits on a plate and pouring milk into a jug; while the tea was brewing she dressed the pot in its cosy for warmth; then carried the pot, the cups, the jug, the sugar bowl and the biscuits into the lounge on a tray.

The boy was sitting on the verge of his seat and looking down at the dog, who sat by the heater staring intently back at him. The dog was small and long-legged, with a rough coat the colour of winter and treacle-coloured eyes, and a spiky moustache of wet whiskers after rummaging in the grass. "What's your dog's name?" the boy asked, without glancing up.

The old lady – whose name was Matilda – put the tray on the little glass table that stood between the chairs, and poured the tea into porcelain cups. "His name is Peake," she said. "Do you take sugar?"

"What sort of dog is he?"

The tea flowed fragrantly from the teapot's spout, the colour of conifer sap. "The proper sort, I suppose. He quarrels with cats and chats with strangers and keeps himself clean. He buries bones and keeps tabs on his enemies and sleeps under my bed. That sort of dog."

Rather sharply, as if he detested having to explain

himself, the boy said, "I meant what breed is he, what kind?"

"Who knows?" Matilda shook her head. "The scruffy kind, the busybody kind, the kind which likes his dinner on time. He's something of everything, the way a dog should be. Do you take sugar?" she asked again.

"I don't know." The boy looked suddenly thin with confusion. "Should I?"

"You would probably prefer it."

"Yes please, sugar," he said, as if he'd known all along.

Matilda stirred sugar into both cups. The milk turned the tea a pressed-rose brown. Quiffs of white steam waltzed and vanished. The boy returned to studying Peake. "You should have called him Max," he said. "Max is a good name for a dog."

"A good name for some dogs," Matilda agreed, "but not for Peake."

"Does he bite?"

"Occasionally, I'm afraid. There are certain cats, and certain people, of whom he particularly disapproves."

The boy smiled – as if he too disapproved of

certain things, and was occasionally tempted to bite them. Peake was watching the visitor closely, neither wagging his tail nor growling but simply staring. He watched the boy take the cup and saucer that Matilda passed across the table; his ears, angular as envelopes, twitched when the spoon clinked on the cup. The boy looked appreciatively into the tea, but pouted when Matilda offered him the biscuit plate. "I prefer biscuits with jam," he said.

"So do I," said Matilda. "There were some in the tin, but I ate them. There's usually only Peake and myself, you see, so we eat all the fancy biscuits and leave the plain ones for last. I'd have bought a cake or some tarts if I'd known we were expecting a visitor today."

The boy only crinkled his nose, and did not apologize for his uninvited presence. He took a biscuit and ate it miserably, as if it were made of clay. While he crunched on the splinters, Matilda closed the door that led to the kitchen and the door which led to the hall, so the lounge room was made snug and private, like the cabin of a boat. Then, with some relief, she settled into her armchair, which was her favourite chair and the one she always sat in, although it was not very different from the one on which the boy perched.

The chairs faced each other with the little table in between, their broad flanks turned away from the television with its piked legs and wooden shell. Every evening Matilda sat in this small square room with Peake, listening to the radio or reading a magazine or playing records on the gramophone. They did not have many visitors, and never any who were children. And yet, although it was completely peculiar to sit in her chair and see a fussy boy sitting opposite her, Matilda somehow felt that things were as they should be. It seemed that she had seen this exact boy sitting exactly where he sat countless times before. She said, "I'm sorry about the biscuits. I wish I had something nice to give you. But you'll be warm soon, and maybe happy."

The boy only shrugged, for he was nearing the age when it is embarrassing to admit you can be happy. Matilda guessed he was eleven or twelve. His hair, which was pale, was fine, and not tidy; there was still enough childhood in him to plump the cheeks of his scowly face. His eyes were lashy, and grey as cinder. He wore a loose red collarless shirt with three unfastened buttons at the throat. It was a flimsy garment for such a damp day – Matilda wondered if his mother had told him to take his coat, but he'd been too vain to obey. His trousers were the colour of charcoal, and showed, on the knees, signs of dirt. On his feet were a pair of cotton socks and good scuffed lace-up boots. He did not smell of anything, yet nor was he perfectly clean. He was not fat or puny, short or tall, dainty or strapping, but medium in all ways, a boy from the illustrations in an annual. He looked the kind who felt cooped up indoors, who preferred to be outside climbing trees and building forts and having sword fights with sticks, who endeavoured to be injured when playing boisterous sports so he could then be nobly brave. He looked the type who'd sooner suffer a painful illness than spend an afternoon drinking tea with an old woman. Matilda liked all these things about him very much. He was like a strong bold bird that had flown into the room and, finding itself cornered, was bored, but unafraid.

Before she could think of anything to say, the visitor lowered his cup, wiped his mouth with his wrist, and regarded her through grave eyes. His voice was grim when he announced, "I have bad news for you."

Matilda had lived for seventy-five years, and she wasn't afraid of bad news. She had heard it before, and she had always survived it, and she'd learned that bad news is part of being alive, and thus should not be resented. Anyway, at seventy-five most news is neither good nor bad, but simply something to accept. She thought she knew what the boy would say, but she bit her lip and kept her thoughts to herself. She wanted to hear how her puzzling guest, with his eccentric etiquette, might put the momentous fact into words. "What is it?"

The boy's grey eyes roamed the room – across the mantel with its clocks and statues, over the walls with their paintings and picture rails, down to where Peake had flattened out before the heater – before returning, like dark clouds, to her. He declared the matter without evasion: "Your house smells like old people."

Matilda blinked, surprised and deflated; her emotions, which had grown grand as a symphony in an instant, fell down like skittles, and she felt a little bereft and nonplussed. But she reminded herself that the boy was only a child, and his childish impudence made her smile. She hesitated several moments to prove she was taking him seriously; then, although she knew the answer, having once been a child herself, she asked, "What do old people smell like?"

"Like coats in mothy cupboards." He winced in revulsion. "Like cold porridge in a bowl. Like taps dripping for years and years. That's how they smell."

Matilda said, "How awful."

"I've been sitting here for ages, waiting for you, almost choking to death!" The boy quaked with frustration. "Why are you like this?" he demanded to know.

"I don't mean to be." Matilda couldn't help laughing, everything was so bizarre. The afternoon was turning out very differently from what she'd imagined. She would not be able to finish reading the novel she'd set aside. "A person gets used to their own smell, I suppose, and doesn't notice it. I should have kept a window open. It's unforgivable to smell like a tap."

"You think it's funny." The boy scowled. "Don't you care? You should hate it – being so wrinkly, walking so slowly, none of your fingers straight. No one looks at you any more, all your colours have gone. Doesn't that make you angry? Doesn't it make you sad? Isn't it horrible, being old?"

Matilda considered her hands, which were dotted with spots and crimped with lines and lumpy with thick veins. Her fingers had once been smooth and white as piano keys. She said, "Being old is sometimes painful, but it isn't horrible. It's just what I am. When I was a girl, I looked in a mirror and saw me. Now I'm old, but when I look in a mirror, the person I see is still me. I'm not graceful or pretty any more, but maybe I am something else – something just as good, or better. Once I was an acorn, now I'm an oak tree."

The boy snorted, unimpressed by trees. "I bet when you were a little girl, you thought old things were horrible."

Tea-leaves floated in a penny-sized pool of tea in the bottom of Matilda's cup. "Everything that's young is troubled by what is old," she admitted. "When I was small, there was an elderly woman who lived at the bend of the road. She never said an unkind word to me, she never even looked at me, but I was frightened of her. She was so withered, so crumpled. I knew she had once been a small girl too, but I couldn't believe it. She was oldness, and nothing else. She was like an abandoned nest you find in a bough, tatty and disintegrating to dust. Even now, the memory of her makes me shiver. It is strange, that oldness is so hard to love or forgive."

"Well, do you love it, now that *you're* old?"

Matilda gazed into her cup. She thought about the child she had been, and the person she was now. When she was young, she had sometimes felt old, as if she'd been born and lived life many times. As she'd grown older, she had often felt as inexperienced and easily fooled as a toddler. Time and wisdom were tricksy things. Hearing the silence, Peake lifted his head and stared at her; then stared long and hard at their visitor before laying his head down again. "Young people think oldness is the bottom of a mountain," Matilda said finally. "In truth, it is the top. I am old, because I have lived a whole life. I have climbed a long, long way. When I look back the way I have come, I can see the town I was raised in, and my mother and father. I see houses I lived in, friends that I made, people and pets that I loved. I see the wrong turns I took, places where I tripped, places where I skipped and sang and ran. I can see for years and years. To have such a view, you have to be standing on top of a mountain. The top is a difficult place to be – it's windy and it's perilous, and lonely sometimes – but it is the top, and there's nowhere else to go."

The boy had curled up on the settee while Matilda spoke, propping his chin on his palm. When she fell silent, he unexpectedly smiled. Smiling curved his eyes into crescents, so he looked like a sunny creature from a birthday card. Matilda guessed he was probably a clever boy, full of wit and curiosity, a thorn in his teacher's side, a ringleader of his friends. When his mother asked him to do something, he did it well, although only after the correct degree of complaint. "Are you warmer now?" she asked.

The boy glanced at the heater, where the row of flames was doing its agitated dance behind spindly metal bars. The dancers were blue and orange, tossing their heads and swinging their hips and kicking up their feet. His nose was no longer pink, and it creased when he shook his head. He raised a hand and pointed, saying, "From the top of the mountain, do you see a girl in a boat?"

On the sideboard behind Matilda stood a brown-and-white photograph glassed inside a silver frame. In the photo, a slim young lady in a long oilskin coat stood at the helm of a spry white boat. The boat's canvas sails were rolled, but a breeze was blowing the girl's dark hair about her shoulders and face. All around the girl and the vessel bucked a playful sea, and the boat was anchored into place at the end of a taut rope. It was impossible to decide if the photograph was a picture of a sailing boat, or the portrait of a girl.

Matilda did not bother turning in her chair – she knew what the photograph looked like. "Yes," she said, "I see that girl. She is the one I see all the time, whether I'm looking for her or not."

"She's you, isn't she?"

"She was me – when I wasn't an acorn or a tree, but somewhere in between."

"Were you a sailor?"

Matilda shrugged. "When you're old, there are a lot of things you have been. A tree is just a single thing, but it has different branches. All the branches are important – all of them make up the tree. On one of my branches, I was a sailor. Although, in truth, more a searcher than a sailor."

"What were you searching for?"

Matilda paused, wanting the right words. "I searched for the answer to a question. I sailed the world trying to find it, and eventually I did. But some answers don't finish a quest – they merely start it. If everything had been finished back then," she told her visitor, "I don't think you would be here."

The boy reached out and took a biscuit, broke it into pieces, and ate it in several resolute bites, as if to show that, now he was here, he did not intend leaving until he was good and ready. "And where would *you* be?" he asked, eyeing her steadily. "Would you be here, sitting in this room, with just a dog to keep you company?"

"Who knows?" Matilda contemplated the walls, the crowd of cold ornaments. "The view from the mountain top is good, but you can only see clearly the road you took to reach where you stand. The other roads – the paths you might have taken, but didn't – are all around you too, but they are ghost roads, ghost journeys, ghost lives, and they are always hidden by cloud."

The boy's grey gaze wandered over her face. In the shallow wrinkles of her skin were whispers of the girl Matilda had been. The boy himself was unmarked and flawless, nobody except himself. "I would like another biscuit," he said sombrely. "I would like more tea."

The dark-haired girl who would stand at the helm of a lean white sailing boat was born in the grandest house of a town that sprawled along a pure-white coastline, its windows turned to the sea. Her parents named her Matilda Victoria Adelaide, but that is a big name for a small girl so almost everyone cut its size down to Maddy. As a child Maddy was slender and silent, yet she was not a delicate thing. She lived what was rather a lonesome life, but she was never filled with pity for herself. She was like a wildflower which grows in what earth it can claim, what

23

sunlight touches it, what rain falls on it, and is grateful and happy. She was like a piece of glass that has been tossed in water for a long time: mysterious but simple, without sharp edges, and not as fragile as it looks.

Her father was an important man, although Maddy wasn't sure what he did that made him so, other than being broad and gruff. She was rather scared of him, though he treated her with the same blunt fairness that he dealt out to all things. Her knowledge that Papa was important made him something to fear, maybe – most important things are also frightening. When she walked with him through town, which she did not often do, Maddy saw that people were pleased to receive Papa's attention – pleased, and also alarmed, like children being noticed by a nun. Maddy knew that her father had lots of money, because he was often away from home earning it. When she was small and her mother said the word "earning", Maddy hadn't understood what she meant. She decided that Mama had meant to say "ironing". So for much of her childhood Maddy believed that her father's job was to heat a great iron on a great stove and to press all the world's paper money flat so it would sit tidily in pockets and in cash-register tills. Such a job would be hot and heavy work, which explained Papa's gruffness as well as his importance. One memorable day the iron man visited her at boarding school, and cut a swathe across the quadrangle with his lofty imperiousness, and took his daughter out of lessons and to a restaurant for lunch; as he climbed into the brougham to leave, he gave Maddy a pound which he had ironed especially flat, which crackled like autumn when she closed it in her hand. She spent the pound immediately, but kept the recollection of that water-smooth note forever – as well as the memory of another gift, the first present Papa ever gave her, a toy felt giraffe that Maddy had desperately loved, that sat on her pillow and watched with beady eyes throughout the years of her growing up until the day when, feeling burdened and stormy and older than she was, Maddy threw it into a bag of castaways that were sent to the underdressed and toyless poor. And afterwards, when the giraffe was gone, Maddy felt more impoverished than anyone who'd ever lived. She had discovered she could be callous and stupid. The discovery of these faults combined with the loss of her toy felt like a mortal wound. She looked at the lovely things that surrounded her, the ribbons and bracelets and necklaces and buckles and silk flowers and china-faced dolls, and none of them were a consolation. She pined for what she had let go. Then and there Maddy vowed that, for the rest of her life, she would hold tightly to what she loved.

The only person who called Maddy by her weighty Matilda-Victoria-Adelaide name was her mother, of whom Maddy was also afraid. As with so many grown-up ladies, Mama seemed to teeter forever on the crumbly threshold of fury. When she was furious, she did not shriek or hurl shoes. Instead she slivered her eyes and turned away, as if her daughter were the most disappointing, most disagreeable, most time-wasting creature in the world. Like her father, Maddy's mother had a job, which was to fret the fate of mites in Foundling Hospitals. The mites were not bugs, but children; the children lived in Hospitals, but not because they were sick. In fact they were too healthy, and their numbers forever increased. Maddy found it all very confusing, but for Mama it was endlessly diverting. She organized money-raising occasions for herself and her friends – trips to the theatre and races, card games, dress-ups, progressive dinners and guest speakers – at which the mysterious mites and their doctorless Hospitals were rarely mentioned and never encountered, yet over whose fates there was nonetheless much fretting done. When she was little, Matilda felt some resentment towards these mites that Mama loved, and thought they should make their own mothers love them, and not steal all the love out of hers.

Once a month Mama stayed overnight in the city, bringing back from its fashionable stores hats and ties and furry cloaks for her husband and daughter so they would always be above criticism. But for her regular forays to the metropolis, Mama would have speedily expired from fresh air and ennui. "It's fine to be a big fish in a small pond," she told her daughter, waving a dismissive hand at the shops and people of their town, "but give this fish the ocean any day." In fact their house was only a short walk from the ocean, but Mama never visited it because the salt played havoc with her hair. As a child, Maddy thought her mother was beautiful, like a unicorn or an ivory carving. Mama laughed with fluty lightness, the way a handkerchief falls. Her nose was as prettily pinched as a thorn. Maddy loved to contemplate her; though not to touch or talk to her. Mama, as Maddy knew her, was blazing and reposeful, chilling and torrid. She was the four seasons put together inside a person. It was hard to know what to say to somebody like that.

When Maddy was home from school, the family ate supper at one end of the shiny dining table. Her parents asked her questions and listened to her, and Maddy tried to be interesting and worthy of their regard. Though she knew she was a small thing in their busy lives, she also knew they loved her as much as they could manage under the circumstances. Maddy had her drawbacks, and at the dinner table she was always heavily aware of them. She wasn't a doll, something Mama could pet and play with; clothes and parties confused her. She wasn't a boy, someone who could stand in the iron man's shadow and learn to be frightening like him. Maddy was, in fact, an overlookable child, doubtful and reluctant in her dealings with others, mousey as a mouse. She was easily hurt, deceived and dispirited. Left to her own devices, however, she was inventive and independent, and smart for her age. Luckily, she was smart enough to realize that her mother and father loved her as much as she needed them to. She wasn't necessary, not like money or the swish city stores: but she did belong, she had a place between her parents, and they would not let her go.

They would not put her in a castaway bag and send her off to the poor. At home Maddy was safe, and she knew it. Just the same, she was a worried child.

The things that worried Maddy worry many children, although each believes that he or she is alone with their woes. She was, for a start, so diffident. There were countless waifish children in town, and at boarding school there were a hundred garrulous girls: but Maddy did not know the complex magic that turns an acquaintance into a friend, so no one was her particular confederate. Nobody bullied her or called her names – but many thought she was a snob, because shyness often looks like haughtiness. Others might have liked to befriend her, yet could find no way of speaking to her. She always seemed as nervy as a foal when approached. Mostly, other children rejected her on the grounds that she was strange, and strangeness among children is despised. In truth, Maddy *was* strange, the way an octopus or an anemone or a goat's eye is strange. She had a perfect right to exist, and she was perfectly made in every way … but she seemed not-quite-right for the world, as if she'd been raised by monkeys or wolves. Part of her longed to be scathing and poised, to whisper in ears and skip a long rope and receive perfumed invitations to parties – and part of her couldn't bear the idea. In her heart, Maddy knew she was good, and that difference is rare and special: the problem was that no one else seemed to think the same. And so she came to understand that she stood apart, and it made her feel important, and unwantedly sad.

She was happiest at home, by herself, on long weekends and holidays. She played with her dolls for days at a time, deep inside their intricate lives of deadly rivalry and adoration. On creamy summer evenings she walked to the beach, stepping through rock-pools with her boots around her neck. She watched crabs digging their evening homes, knelt on the pier to see stingrays sweep the shallows. On scorching afternoons she roamed the hills, pressing her hands to the trunks of eucalypts, picking cockatoo feathers from the grass. She watched bull ants marching off to battle and mahogany snakes sleeping on stones. Rabbits thumped the cracked earth, the hot air tasted like medicine. The gum trees were friendly to her, nodding their olive heads. Bark peeled from them, brittle as cicada shell; in their branches stood tawny frogmouths, their beaks lordishly raised. In red shadows cast by rocky cliffs lived a nargun, who was also her friend. Shambling, old as the hills, larger than a draught horse, the nargun emerged from its cave snarling, its clawed feet crushing the leaf litter, the stink of stagnant water fuggy in its coat. Its tongue would flicker from its hideous head as it told her where an echidna lay buried, a fox was crouched. The nargun's eyes were bigger than top hats, its body groaned when it moved. Despite its size, it was a swift and formidable hunter; it dined on bullocks ambushed at waterholes, and it snacked on unpleasant young ladies. Maddy wished she could ride the nargun to school – across the quadrangle and up the staircase and into the classroom. She heard the floor splinter beneath its terrible weight, saw her classmates fleeing like mice. She lay on her back telling the creature her troubles, and the nargun unlatched its scarlet mouth like a trapdoor to growl, "If no one cares for you, care for no one in return." And under the brilliant sun, surrounded by trees, deafened by insects and dry with thirst, this sounded like excellent advice. Maddy didn't need anyone. She could live by herself in the bush, and nothing would matter to her.

In the daylight Maddy believed this, and many dramatic things besides. In the black of night, however, she was wrung with fear. She did not want to be un-caring, and uncared-for. She did not want to spend her whole life taking steps in the darkest, the coldest, the most lonely direction. Yet how, she wondered, does one craft sturdy happiness out of something as im-portant, as complicated, as unrepeatable and as easily damaged as a life?

One evening when Maddy was neither a little girl nor a lady but something gangly in-between, her father lay his knife and fork on his plate, wiped his hands on his napkin, and smiled across the dining table at her. His black eyes were sparkling, which they did when he had something clever in mind. "Matilda Victoria Adelaide," he said, "I hear you have now finished school."

This was true: Maddy had just that afternoon caught the train home from boarding school for the final time. She had climbed the stairs to her bedroom and unpacked her suitcase onto her bed, and had stood staring down at the workbooks she no longer needed, unsure what she was meant to do next. She had felt a lake-like emptiness, the stillness of a held breath. She knew that something must happen, but had no clue what it must be. "I have, Papa," she said.

"Excellent," said her father. "That's the most tiresome part over and done. So, after all that history and geography and elocution and needlework, did you learn the answer?"

Maddy blinked twice. "Which answer, Papa?"

Her father poured the last of the wine into his glass, and motioned for the maid to bring the port. "The answer to the only important question there is, of course: *What is the world's most beautiful thing?*"

Mama, opposite Maddy, leaned on her elbows and gave a languorous laugh. "That's easy, Matilda," she said. "Victory is the world's most beautiful thing. There's nothing uglier than defeat, and nothing prettier than winning. Don't ask the girl ridiculous questions, Frank."

Papa smiled at his wife with cool patience. "Maddy, allow me to clarify. What is the world's most beautiful thing, *apart from victory*?"

Maddy looked back at him, the cutlery stilled in her hands. The world's most beautiful thing: was her father serious, could there be such a thing? Maddy had never known the iron man to joke, or to say or do something that had no meaning. Indeed, she sensed that this was a vital moment, that her father expected nothing less than that she dive deep inside herself for the answer. Her response would be a measure of her, something he wouldn't forget. She thought for a minute, her hands cramping into fists. There were so many beautiful things in the world – in the dining room alone there were dozens. The chandelier in the ceiling was dazzling. The tiles of the hearth were charming. The smell of roast beef was divine. On a cushion in a corner sat her little black cat Perseus, whose Egyptian face was finer than a chip of onyx. Maddy thought about all she had seen in her sixteen years of life – the city and the ocean, the hills arranged round the town. She had seen trees and earth and animals, and the sky in its various blue-black moods. From among these things, she selected carefully. "I think," she said, "that sea-eagles are the most beautiful things in the world."

"Sea-eagles!" Papa guffawed, slapping his palm on the table-top so the wine in the glasses jumped. "Ten

years of the best education, and you give me an angry chicken? Think again, Maddy."

Maddy flinched, feeling a wobble of panic: she had disappointed him. Nevertheless, she was the iron man's daughter, and she had inherited a touch of his stubborn pride. She pretended to think harder, but mulishly fetched up the same reply: "Sea-eagles."

Her father smiled to see himself in her; then he rolled his expensive eyes, which had already seen countless gorgeous things and intended to see more. "It's commendable that you stand by your convictions, Maddy," he said, "yet your answer makes me fear your mind is quite provincial. Now your schooling is over it's time you learned a thing or two. We can't have you wandering round with a dishcloth for a brain. Before the week is out, you and I will be embarking on a journey around the world," he informed his child. "It will not be a holiday or a grand tour, but a working expedition. We will make it our duty to see everything upon which human eyes should rightly feast. And when we have witnessed them all, you will tell me what is, without doubt, the most beautiful thing in the world."

"Don't forget to bring me back a present," said Mama, bone-wearily.

So within the week Maddy found herself following her father up the busy gangway of a steamer, her trunk being heaved aboard by sailors, her hat threatening to depart on the coal-dusted wind. Excitement tingled inside her, making everything vibrant and loud. At sixteen she was willowy, not too tall, and dreamy-eyed; her skin was dusky and unlined, her nose a little snubbed. Her chestnut hair reached to her elbows when not bundled up and pinned. On the outside, Maddy was changing into someone new, someone to whom gentlemen doffed their hats and shopkeepers spoke respectfully; inside, however, she was still the hushed and perplexed girl she had always been. She still felt bitterly her own awkwardness. But as she hurried up the steep gangway Maddy knew that her life, which had until now been closed like a bud, was finally beginning to unfurl. She would soon see for herself the colours that were sunk into life's petals and leaves.

Papa had planned an itinerary which took the pair

of them circling the globe. Quickly they settled into a routine. They would disembark in an exotic city on the edge of a continent, find transport in the form of a carriage or train, hire a guide who was familiar with the language and sites: and then they would begin their search, criss-crossing the land, hunting out treasures, poring over maps, arguing and discussing and comparing the merits of the spectacles which stood before them. Maddy had brought a journal, the biggest and thickest she could find: nonetheless she had to make her writing tiny, her sketches miniatures, to squeeze in all her meditations on the wonders she saw. On their mission to discover the world's most beautiful thing, she and her father visited cathedrals as tall as alps, and stood in reverence beneath painted domes capping Heaven above their heads. They saw mosques and temples and ivy-tangled graveyards, took side-trips to deserts to see colossal Buddhas hewn from mountainsides and to soundless monasteries in the middle of nowhere to kneel before relics of saints. They strolled down the gilded halls of palaces and castles, climbed the stone steps of turreted towers, felt the mist of fountains and orange groves. Stained-glass windows in time-honoured university halls smudged them with blurs of light. They walked in circles through mighty libraries, humbled by how much there was to know. They attended plays and symphonies, and readings of poetry. Each evening they ate a foreign meal, and each night they slept like the dead.

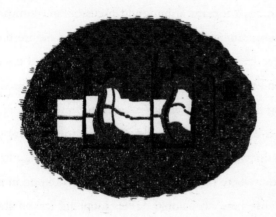

To Maddy's surprise, her father made an excellent touring companion. She had expected him to be supercilious or disparaging, but it seemed the iron man had stayed at home. In his place stood a man Maddy did not know, someone adventurous and appreciative and patient. At first Maddy couldn't think what to say to him, for they were strangers; but as the weeks and months passed they became one another's closest friend, sharing the same memories, knowing things about each other that none but the other one knew. Maddy had always respected her father, but now she decided she loved him too. Loving him made her feel merry, and wishfully sad. She didn't want their journey to end – she wanted to keep her adventurous Papa forever – she could not bear the thought of going home and seeing him stiffen into the stern and preoccupied iron man. She would feel robbed and deserted. Lying on a narrow bed in her compartment of a train, the metal wheels screeching on the icy tracks as a gale howled across the tundra outside, Maddy shut her new, preferred father inside the prison of her heart, from where he could not escape. She would never stop loving him; she would never doubt his love for her. He might age, alter, spoil, disappear: but for Maddy he would always be this happy-go-lucky travelling man, changeless on his pedestal, preserved like a flower pressed inside a thick book.

Together they visited scientific laboratories, and peered into microscopes to see a drop of blood made monstrous; at planetariums they looked through gigantic telescopes at pin-point planets and stars. They meandered the length of galleries and museums and acres of botanic gardens, reading aloud from the plaques which accompanied each masterpiece and fossil and shrub. In glasshouses they inspected fungi and ferns, and sniffed prize-winning blooms. They drank from goblets in the shade of kasbahs, and spent afternoons in extravagant bazaars unrolling rugs which had taken decades to weave. They visited kilns to gaze into bulbs of molten glass. They climbed to the point of a pyramid and breathed, at the summit, the dust of millenniums. At the edge of an archaeological dig they witnessed the unearthing of a pharaoh entombed for thousands of years. Maddy imagined his royal spirit, disturbed, winging like a dark bat into the sky.

For her seventeenth birthday her father gave her a smooth brass kaleidoscope. Maddy, squinting down its length, saw chips of colour swimming in remarkable patterns. She sat on a palazzo balcony of a city built on a sea, woozy with the richness of the wonders she'd seen. She felt such admiration for humankind's artistry and nature's glory that she was frequently speechless, and close to tears. The whole world was a ravishing marvel, there was nothing that wasn't fabulous to her – the cracks between cobbles, the coldness of ice, the greenness of apples, the squeak of soldiers' boots.

When the diggers uncovered his time-lost face, Maddy had thought the desiccated, eyeless, mummified pharaoh exquisite enough to rival the bluest lake.

She climbed sliding dunes in the footsteps of her father, and stared across shifting deserts as her ankles were peppered by burning beads of sand. She hiked with him to the mouths of volcanoes and gazed into flaming maws. Lava roiled in scarlet clouds at their heels, boiling the breath in their lungs. They skated on frozen, flake-dappled ponds in the shadow of snow-iced mountain peaks. They picked a path between slippery glaciers, and watched a stately parade of icebergs part the grey ocean. They shouted into canyons older than dinosaurs, as wide and deep as sea beds, and heard their words shouted back at them. They explored valleys that hid steaming rainforests, and jungles shot through with rainbowed birds. They fumbled along limestone caves to see uncanny stalagmites and stalactites, they crawled into underground caverns to find crystals embedded in boulders. They hired a boat and rowed themselves around psychedelic coral reefs, the water as tepid as a bath and the colour of kitten eyes. They bowed at the feet of the highest and most merciless pinnacle in the world. Their cheeks were

dampened, their ears were deafened, by the spray and
tumultuous roaring of a hundred waterfalls. They
stood in the flying, flickering midst of a million
migrating butterflies.

On the evening
of her eighteenth birthday, Maddy
opened her journal and made a list of the jewels
and precious stones she'd held. *Gold, diamond, emerald;*
ruby, turquoise, pearl; amber, jade, marble … there were
some she had forgotten. Beneath these she listed what
she thought were the most perfect tastes and smells.
Coffee, cinnamon, peaches; vanilla, honey, basil; baking
bread, fresh bread, toasting bread. She could not list everything. She thought of the magnificent animals she
had seen in aquariums and zoos. *Tigers, hammerheads,*

crocodiles; cheetahs, flamingos, timber wolves; gazelles, polar bears, Arabian horses, and dozens and dozens more. She felt suddenly tired, and lay her head on the desk. She was filled to the brim with beauty, and it was as heavy as lead. For two years Maddy had been steeped in the world's sumptuousness, and it had left her feeling as if she had stayed too long at an extravagant feast. At that moment she craved simplicity, something simple like a fish or a stone, a pale room with nothing in it, and silence for a year.

Her father knocked on the cabin door. He was dressed, for the last time, in his travelling clothes – linen shirt and trousers and vest, a plume of gold cravat at his throat – for they were not far from the coast of home. Tomorrow morning their ship would dock, and their quest would be at an end. "Happy birthday, Matilda!" he said in his loud voice, and gave his daughter a parcel wrapped in paper and a bow. "Before you open your present," he said, "you must tell me the answer. What, besides a sea-eagle, is the most beautiful thing in the world?"

"There is no answer to your question, Papa," Maddy replied. She had prepared herself for this moment, and she would not change her mind. "I have looked and looked, and thought and thought, but there is no answer. There's so much that is sublime in the world, but it is splendour that should not be compared. Each beautiful thing is supremely, absolutely beautiful. There's nothing that is lovelier than everything else combined."

The father considered his child. If he was disappointed, it did not show. If he was pleased, that did not show either. He said, "Perhaps you need to look more closely at what is right under your nose."

With that he kissed her forehead and brusquely left the cabin, as if he had remembered something imperative he needed to do. Maddy, listening to his footsteps thump away down the corridor, longed to call him back to her, to have a few final moments with the father alongside whom she had criss-crossed the globe. She would have the memory of him, but the truth is that a memory is hardly ever good enough to console a heart.

She looked down at the parcel in her lap, and unwrapped it carefully. Amid many layers of tissue was a small, silver-handled mirror. Maddy held it up so she could see her reflection, her dark eyes and freckled cheekbones. *I am the most beautiful thing in the world.*

Her eyes filled with silly tears, which she dashed with a scoffing laugh. She knew she wasn't lovely, not like a saluki or a palace or a Ming vase. She was no princess from a storybook. But she was well-read and widely travelled now, and she'd pondered interesting things. She still felt misfitted and out-of-place, like a jigsaw piece cut wrong; but it no longer caused her grief to feel that way. Now, she was pleased she hadn't changed to become like everyone else. Her courage and defiance made her father proud of her – it made her beautiful. Gazing into the mirror at her ordinary face, her ordinary nose and mouth, Maddy knew she wasn't a fairy princess, and that she wouldn't live a fairytale life; but she would find her own way, and she would be all right.

The boy was prowling around the lounge room, considering closely the curious objects which decorated the shelves and walls. He brushed his fingers over the opalescent wings of insects blown from Venetian glass. He held an Amazonian mask to his face, and grumbled through its fanged mouth. On the floor was a lustreless Persian rug across which fantastic creatures challenged and cavorted; on the wall behind the television hung a cresting Japanese sea. The antimacassars were Irish, embroidered with fat clover. On the windowsill lay a walrus carved by an Inuit from tusk.

Beside it stood a buffalo whittled by an Indian chief, who many moons ago had given Matilda a secret name he'd written in ash. There were leather-bound books from England and samovars from Siberia and corn ladies from Mexico; there were tikis from hot Hawaii, and penguin skulls stripped clean by Antarctic winds. Peake's amber glare followed the boy everywhere, the self-appointed guardian of the museum. The visitor found a plump wooden doll inside which hid a smaller wooden doll, and another inside that, and another. He held the tiniest doll in his palm sceptically; then turned to Matilda and asked, "Why do you have so many things?"

Matilda smiled. "Objects remind people of their lives, I suppose. So many things change with time, so much disappears. It's good to see something that was there, in the past, and hasn't changed since. That looks and feels exactly as it did on the day it became important."

The boy's lip curved, he seemed unconvinced. He put the nesting dolls back together and resumed his tour of the room. He probably owned nothing, hardly more than his clothes – a few special and shiny things, perhaps, which had no weight and could be hidden in a hand. There was lightness in that, Matilda supposed; and felt a twinge of envy. This room and its untold souvenirs was like a memorial, a bell jar. Everything she owned spoke of what had been – never about what might have been, or what may yet be. The boy stopped suddenly at the window, peeping between the slats of the blind. It was the beginning of spring, when night still comes early, tamping down the late afternoon. Already the lawn and garden and the street beyond were dim. The lounge room was cosy now, but it looked dank and cold outside. "Is someone expecting you home for dinner?" she asked, only to hear what he would say.

The boy shook his head imperceptibly. He would not be drawn into such discussions. He said, "You should have kept that toy giraffe."

"I know—"

"If you had kept that, maybe you wouldn't need all these things. You have these things, but they're not what you want. Is that what life is – settling for what you can get, if you can't have what you really want? A pile of junk, instead of the one perfect thing? Pictures inside your head, instead of the real thing in your hands?"

Something like a strap of metal tightened around Matilda's chest. "Sometimes," she conceded. "For many people, often it is. Life is a lot longer and more complicated than you expect it to be. Nothing is permanent and certain. Every day you have to renegotiate a way to survive the hours between waking up, and falling sleep… You're an odd child, aren't you?" She looked at him over the rim of her glasses. "You do and say some strange things."

The boy replied, with much gravitas, "I am what I am."

Matilda said, "Well, I am in need of more tea."

"Wait!" Her guest spun on his heels. His ash-coloured eyes were familiar to her, as was his fawn frown. "I have a question. Did you really believe what you thought on the last day of your quest? Did you really think that you were going to be all right?"

Matilda thought back through the years that separated herself from the girl on a steamer holding a mirror in her hand. "Yes," she said, "I did. I had to. I knew I wouldn't live a fairytale life. And for that very reason I had to have faith in myself, just as does a princess in a fairytale. I had to believe there was worth, and courage, and promise in me. How else could I have lived? How else could I have survived what was going to happen next?"

The boy lifted his pointy chin, looking down his nose at her. "What's going to happen?"

"Two very important things." Matilda stood up from her chair with difficulty. "Peake is going to get his dinner, and I am going to make another pot of tea."

It is always a peculiar feeling to be home after a long time away. Maddy had missed her bedroom and her little cat Perseus, and she was glad to see these again. But the house she'd always lived in, the town where she had been born – these didn't feel to Maddy like things she knew and loved. Everything about them seemed cloistered and monochrome. Waking every morning to the same things, she discovered that she missed journeying, knowing that each day would take her somewhere she had never been. And she missed her father, who, as soon as their ship sighed into port, went straight back to ironing money – as if, through all the months of excitement and discovery, through every hour of his epic search for breathtaking beauty with her, ironing was what he'd secretly wished he could do. The iron man hurried about, making up for lost time – time that had been given over to his daughter, and was thus classified as lost. Maddy had expected things to be this way, and reminded herself that Papa loved her and she him, yet she couldn't help feeling piqued. Her travelling father, Maddy thought reproachfully, could have tried a little harder to stay.

Shockingly, Maddy hadn't missed her mother while she was abroad, and what pleasure there was in seeing her again was speedily rubbed away. Maddy had grown up during her travels, and had cultivated some grown-up likes and dislikes. She knew how she wanted to dress, and how to style her hair. She knew what she wanted to eat, and when she'd eaten enough. She had her own convictions, and the pluck to almost always defend them. She arrived home feeling like a proper person – but her mother swept her up like a stray puppy from the street. When Mama looked at Maddy, she saw that her daughter's hair was too long, and worn in a style that didn't suit. The clothes Maddy preferred did not flatter her shape. Maddy could bene-fit from pinching, plucking, perfuming, and some powder on her sunbeaten cheeks. Matilda Victoria Adelaide was a girl on the brink of personal and social catastrophe, she had come home just a hair's-breadth away from being Frankenstein's monster, and Mama was aghast. Everywhere she turned, the year's most desirable beaux were being snatched up like trout by lesser girls, and it smarted. "I'm embarrassed!" Mama declared. "Embarrassed! Imagine: *my* daughter, left on the shelf like a bowl of last night's custard. My daughter! I cannot believe it is happening."

And yet, it was hardly surprising. Invited to parties, Maddy stood in a corner radiating disgruntlement. She hated the smothersome dresses her mother chose; she had no clue what to say to the beaux who sidled up to her. She had only her travels to talk about, and she wouldn't share them with people she didn't like. Standing mute, she felt ridiculous, and very near to tears. "But you needn't say anything!" Mama wailed, after yet another evening spent in futile son-in-law pursuit. "You'll have plenty of time to talk when your best days are behind you. Forget talking, Matilda – girlhood is for smiling. Just smile, smile, smile!" So Maddy smiled, and it was the smile of a jellyfish. It got her nowhere, and she didn't care. She was scorning of the fulsome young men she met, and irritated by the competitive young ladies. The parties vexed her, the chatter was infantile, the music made her angry. She didn't care if everyone in the room ignored her – she was glad of it! She longed to be far away, in the middle of the ocean, rambling and unbothered, seeking lovely things. Earthbound, Maddy felt shipwrecked. Her whole world had become torment, and she was the most tormented and tormenting thing in it.

The only time she felt like her old self again was when she was climbing the hills. Whenever she could, Maddy escaped her mother's noisy chagrin and fled into the wilderness. She had missed the hills when she was away, their bushfire smell and crackliness, the still air between the trees. She'd missed seeing lizards vanish under stones, missed hearing bellbird calls link the eucalypts like silver neck chains. She walked the dirt tracks that wove down to the cove, trying to think about nothing. Her mind was crammed with bric-a-brac, teetering and full of sharp corners: it was restful to close a door on the chaos. On the days when her mind couldn't help but think, Maddy thought about what might happen. According to her mother, Maddy should select a gentleman, fence him off with a wedding ring, and embark on a life of glossiness as quickly as possible. It was what well-bred girls were born to do; it was what Mama's ideal daughter would have done at least a year ago. Yet the prospect of such a life made Maddy feel choked. She didn't want to be a pricey bauble, a walking, talking, well-fed decoration. "I want my life to be mystifying," she declared, although she didn't know what she meant.

Sometimes, when the nargun had risen from the banks of a billabong to trudge through the bushland beside her, Maddy discussed love. Though she had packed up her dolls and childhood toys long ago, the nargun remained her confidant and defender. The nargun had no sense of humour, so it never laughed at her; she told it what she dreamt and feared, and it took what she said very seriously. It folded her secrets against its solid black heart and carried their weight for her. "I wouldn't mind if someone fell in love with me," she admitted to the creature. "It might be nice. But he would have to be handsome, and have lustrous hair. He would have to be profound, but never be a bore. He would be generous, but naturally not a wastrel. Clever, but never tedious; clean, but not fussy; careful, but never a prig. He would desperately need me, but also want me to be free. He would be a free-spirit too, of course, but he would always come home to me."

"Such a man does not exist," growled the knowledgeable nargun. "No one is perfect. You are not."

Maddy broke off a gum leaf, and breathed its steely scent. "I suppose you're right," she said, dropping the leaf with a sigh. "If such a man did exist, he would only make me look foolish and mean. Oh, what am I going to do, nargun?" And she felt the familiar panic of staring into a future that unnerved her, and which she didn't understand.

The nargun's clawed feet left rips in the ground from which winged ants swarmed in their thousands. "Perhaps you are meant to be alone," it murmured.

"Your father said you are beautiful. Most beautiful things are alone, in one way or another."

And although she snorted and said, "I'm not beautiful," something in Maddy secretly believed she was. "Is that true?" she asked, and saw herself alone, like a quoll or a cat, living a mysterious life in treetops, eventually forgetting how to speak.

She was indulging in these opulent ruminations when she stepped off the track and onto the beach, and immediately saw the young man. He was crouching at the water's edge, where the waves rolled their foamy knuckles into the sand and left behind a scum of whey-grey bubbles. In his arms he held a great white pelican, whose long yellow bill was affectionately tousling his hair. Maddy stopped at the sight, and a small startled sound yipped out of her. Instantly the pelican lifted its head and found her, fixing her with a single black eye. It lowered its beak to the young man's ear and clacked a sea-bird noise. Immediately the man released the bird, which took to the sky on vast black-and-white wings, the air whumping under it. Maddy watched it tilt across the shallows, its head tucked into its shoulders, its bill a jousting lance. When she looked again at the man, he was staring coolly at her. She tugged her straw hat more securely onto her head. "I'm so – sorry," she said haltingly.

The young man said nothing; as he stood, Maddy saw how boyhood still played around him, that he was about the same age as herself. He was slim but not lanky, and his skin was sunbrowned. His hair fell dishevelled onto his shoulders, the colour of a palomino's tail. He was wearing a pair of tatty red trousers that were cut off at the knees and faded almost to pink. But for a dusting of dry sand, his chest, arms and shins were bare. Maddy had never seen so much of a man, and she didn't know where to look. The young man, however, did not seem discomforted: he stood in silence and considered her, confident as a magpie. The cove was an empty one, rocky and windswept, useless for fishing and swimming, and there was none but the two of them on it, now that the pelican was gone. The heat beat down on the rumpled white dunes, the water lapped the beach with its shushed, encouraging sound. Maddy supposed she should turn and walk away briskly, perhaps alert her mother and other guardians of propriety to the existence of this stranger. Instead she stepped closer, her shoes denting the sand. "I didn't mean to interrupt," she said. "You were talking to that pelican."

Nearer, she saw he had eyes that were smoky, lips that were pale, and long black eyelashes. He seemed about to reply that birds do not speak, or at least not to anyone other than their own kind – instead he smiled, although hardly at all. His gaze travelled seriously down to her feet, and up to her face again. "It doesn't matter," he said, and his voice was trim, a bird's flying wing. "It wasn't saying anything important."

"…They talk about the weather, I suppose?"

"Sometimes. Mostly they talk about wharfs."

Maddy smiled; she didn't laugh. She looked at the young man, and had the singular sensation of being suspended by strings. She felt the sand eroding under her feet, heard the waves repeat a word again and again. The sun was searing, almost stunning, the air was dry as flame. There was a tornado in her, but she hovered inside its calm, quiet centre. "I've never seen you before," she said. "Where have you come from?"

He answered, "Here and there."

"Oh! Me too." A corner of her mind was already noticing his peculiarities, his smokiness, his featheriness, the glint of his skin. There was something impossible, unexpectable, about him. Maddy felt a touch feverish, she wondered if she should sit down. She listened to herself say, "For two years I searched everywhere for the world's most beautiful thing."

Any of the beaux would have gallantly replied, *You, Miss Maddy, if I may say so, are the world's most beautiful thing.* The pelican-boy only said, "There is nothing that's more beautiful than everything else in the world."

If he knew that her heart jumped inside her chest – if he heard her blood sing, if he saw the debris tumble from her mind to leave her whole world clear – he did not show it. He only scuffed the sand with his toes and looked out over the waves. He showed no sign of noticing that time stood still when he said, "If I had to choose one thing – if choosing was the rule – I would choose a sea-eagle. Sea-eagles are the most beautiful things in the world."

He might have had a proper name, but she always called him Feather. She liked to remember the sight of him with the great white bird in his arms. She sensed that, like a rambling sea-bird, he had travelled many blue miles with nothing to guide him except the sun and moon. He walked the water's edge like a wrecked and lost ocean bird which must wait for the wind to recollect it and carry it elsewhere. A stranded, migrating winged thing: when she asked where he came from, Feather would smile and shrug; when she asked if he meant to return to that place, he would simply smile again. His silence made Feather the smartest and most mysterious person Maddy had ever known.

That first afternoon, she walked home from the cove feeling giddy, his image a bright gem in her mind. Her mother and father were surprised to hear their taciturn daughter laugh. She woke early the next morning, when the sun was scarcely up, no longer laughing but filled with disquiet, certain he would be gone. She realized then that she would always feel this way: vulnerable to his loss. "Vulnerability is what love is," she told the nargun, which was breathing under her bed. She finally understood why none of the beaux had ever won her affection. She had been waiting for Feather, and she had not even known.

That morning she went down to the beach running, then walking, then slowing – and running. Stepping past the trees, she did not see him, and the excitement in her heart congealed into a pool of bitterness. She hated herself for hoping he would be there, hated him for not being there. And then she saw him, in the distance, spare as a shadow on the sand; her heart began to thump again. When she came nearer, he showed her a sea-snail suctioned to his finger. She had brought a bottle of lemonade for him, and he pulled the cork with his teeth.

Maddy went to the cove every morning after that, lacing up her walking shoes and setting off into the scrub without telling her mother or the house-maid where she was going. Every day, the first glimpse of Feather on the shore was like the taste of honey on hot bread. He often sat watching the ocean, his knees drawn up under his chin. The breeze sprinkled his shoulders with sparkly grains of sand. Water-bugs would run across his brown feet, and he never brushed them away. Occasionally, hurrying from the trees, she would find him surrounded by seagulls. The birds browsed peacefully, close to him — some of them dozed in the narrow shade that leaned away from his back. They flew off crying the instant they saw her, and Feather would turn his head. It panged her that he could not fly with them, that he was left so alone — yet at the same time she was glad he was weighted to the ground. She always brought small gifts when she visited, sugar biscuits and bottles of cider hidden in her sleeves. In exchange for these presents, one day she asked, "Won't you tell your birds to stay?" Because it seemed to her that nothing could be nicer than to sit beside Feather in the cloudy midst of the gulls.

But Feather shook his head. "Why would I make them stay," he asked, "when they want to go?"

"I wouldn't harm them," Maddy said, ashamed.

"I know it," Feather replied. "They know it too. But it is their nature to fly. It is what they need. You can't make them forget that."

"That's not what I meant," she muttered – disappointed, wishing he'd understood.

Feather looked at her closely, closer than he had looked before. "But I will stay," he said.

That night Maddy lay in bed wondering if *I will stay* is another way of saying *this is where I want to be*. She knew nothing for certain about love, about the words love liked to use. But she felt she was lying in a hammock of gorgeous blossoms, that the world had forgotten everything except her. Her thoughts travelled over his skin, his mouth, rose with his chest as he breathed. *I am yours, you are mine, I will stay.* "Make it true," she whispered secretly, so only the soundless nargun overheard.

The boy sitting in Matilda's lounge room on the flowery settee squirmed into a mortified ball. "Don't say this!" he cried, wriggling his feet and clapping his hands to his ears. "I don't want to hear about things like this!"

Matilda laughed too, at her elderly self and her younger self, and at the blushing boy. "But you should hear about it. This is important. Love is a very important thing in this world."

"Love is horrible! It's stupid!"

Peake was on his four feet, looking angry, his envelope-ears pricked on his scrappy head; Matilda, for the first time in such a long time remembering everything so clearly, thought she might die smiling. Those days on the beach had been, perhaps, the sweetest of her life. She chuckled across the coffee table at the boy, who had pressed his palms over his eyes. "You're right," she said. "Love can be horrible for those who aren't in it. Sometimes it's even horrible for those who are. Love isn't always a good thing, or even a happy thing. Sometimes it's the very worst thing that can happen. But love is like moonlight or thunder, or rain on a tin roof in the middle of the night: it is one of the things in life that is truly worth knowing."

The boy moaned and groaned in pain, digging his fingers into his eyes. Eventually he lowered his hands and slowly unknotted his limbs. "All right," he said flatly, averting his sights. "You can tell me if you have to. But hurry up."

...The world changes when something in it is loved. Words become feeble. Colours glow. Every moment vibrates with possible importance. And the heart that loves wonders how it lived, in the past, without loving – and how it will live now, now that it loves.

Maddy's mind, which had for so long been as teeming as Aladdin's cave, was empty, but for him. Feather was all that mattered, the single essential thing in the world. She thought about him ceaselessly, she couldn't chase him from her mind, not when being introduced to a duchess, not when spiked by a brooch, not when turning the last cards in Patience, not when crossing herself in church. Sitting at the table with Mama and Papa, Maddy didn't taste her dinner – she thought about him. Every hopeful beau flailed inconsequently in comparison to him. Blanketed snugly in bed, she wondered: was he cold, wherever he was? Were the night sounds making him scared? Did he have a coat for cool mornings, did he have enough to eat? Was he lying awake in the dark somewhere, thinking about her? What if he was? What if he wasn't?

Every day was the same; every day was different. Some mornings she found him walking the sandbar or sitting on rocks cracking mussel shells, and sometimes she searched the length of the beach and couldn't find him anywhere. He left no footprints in the dunes, no messages dug into sand. Standing on the deserted beach, Maddy would fight down her dismay, reminding herself that Feather was free – and that so, too, was she. She was still herself, the misfit who regretted she hadn't been raised by wolves. A vision of Feather sipping tea in a drawing-room, surrounded by coy ladies who were tweaking his hair, would creep up on her and make her breathless, and she'd stamp it out like fire. The nargun read her thoughts, and laughed satirically. "You do not seem free to me," it said. "Your heart is a prison, and you are locked in it too."

But most days Maddy's life was worth living, because he was there. Sometimes she tried to see him before he saw her, to catch him at his wildest. As the bush track changed from dirt to sand, she would slow down and step silently. She didn't think of it as spying – rather, it was as if she were still on her quest for beautiful things. She'd crept through jungles to see jaguars, she'd sat like a statue by waterholes while gazelles found the nerve to drink: this was the same. Hidden behind tree trunks and leaves, Maddy watched Feather dreaming, waking, falling asleep. She saw the ocean romp up to him and sweep around his knees. She saw him walk through water, the waves licking his hands, while all about him surged a shoal of tussling fish.

She saw him resting like Pan in a bed of leaves, knowing that if she were closer she would smell the fresh-hay scent of him, smell the ocean and all that grows in it.

He watched the highdives of spear-faced gannets, and she watched him watching them. Mostly, though, she watched him sitting motionless, studying the horizon. Maddy wondered what he was looking for, and what would happen if he saw it. It would be something that would harm her, she sensed, something she didn't understand. *Look away*, she wanted to beg, *look away*.

Maddy would never forget the moment when all the loveliness she'd seen on her travels around the world crumbled into insignificance – when she knew for certain that Feather, homeless on the beach, tousled and tameless as a flash of lightning, was the most beautiful thing in the world. Cathedrals were ruins, compared to him. Stained-glass windows were mud. Only undiscovered rainforests came close to being as beautiful as he. In this moment Maddy saw there was something *miraculous* about him: miraculous like the sun returning each morning, miraculous like a living bird inside a lifeless shell, miraculous like the way rain can turn a dead world green.

It happened on a day like most others. She hadn't known Feather for very long, although it seemed a long time, and she wished it was. Maddy had stepped onto the beach unseen, as she had done many times before. Feather was sitting on the sand and considering the clouds, as she'd seen him do so often. Apart from his hair jinking on the breeze, he sat as still as stone. The ocean itself, with its succession of waves, seemed more likely to stand up and walk than did he. Maddy paused in the shadows, not wanting to disturb him – longing, at the same time, to run to him, fall against him, hold his wrists very tightly, bite her fingernails into him. A fleck appeared in the blue distance, catching her eye; as it drew nearer, the fleck became a petrel. Maddy watched the bird come closer and closer until finally it swooped steeply to the ground and skipped across the sand to Feather. In its beak it held a wan sardine. Feather thanked the bird, took the fish between his fingers, and swallowed the sardine in a gulp.

Maddy gasped. She knew then that she would certainly die without him. Hearing her, Feather looked around. He was not always a gentleman, so he didn't stand. His grey eyes squinted, he shaded them with a hand, and when he saw her he smiled.

"Hello," he said. "I was hoping you would come."

She crossed the sand and knelt beside him. "Have you missed me?"

"Yes," he admitted, "but not much."

She smiled, because *not much* seemed another way of saying *I love you*. She had done nothing loveable – she'd talked to him and listened to him and told jokes and bad stories about herself; she had sat with him while the sun set, she'd let her love for him shine in her eyes – and yet, Maddy was suddenly sure that he loved her.

The petrel had scuttled to the water's edge, fearful. Feather called it to him and it returned cautiously. When it was close enough to touch, it puffed out its chest and plumped down in the sand, allowing her to stroke its sooty head. In exchange for such trust, Maddy spoke about the nargun that protected her, and about things she had seen in remarkable corners of the world. When the breeze blew her hat sideways, Feather smoothed back a fluttering strand of her hair.

That afternoon Maddy went home and informed her mother and father that she was in love with a wild man who dined on raw fish.

★   ★   ★

"Ha!" The boy on the settee jumped out of his slouch, wagging his finger at Matilda. His face was lit as a child's face always is, when he sees and understands something to which everyone else seems ignorant and blind. "*You're* going to be in trouble!"

"How did you guess?" asked Matilda. "It never occurred to me."

Mama and Papa were amused by their daughter's unexpected news. "Feather who?" Mama enquired, flopping like a length of satin across her chaise longue, fanning her face with a manicured hand. "I've never heard of anyone Feather. It doesn't sound like a particularly good family. Sounds like a tribe of dustmen, if you ask me."

"How does he earn his money?" the iron man asked, jocular and lazy after a big lunch, determined not to leave all the twitting to his wife. "Stealing leftovers? Raiding picnics?"

Maddy looked from one to the other, disappointed to feel herself crestfallen. She should have expected this reception, yet her happy heart had not. The air in the library seemed suddenly thick to breathe. From walls between bookcases her ancestors glowered accusingly at her. "Feather doesn't need money, Papa," she said. "He spends all day at the beach."

"All day at the beach?" Mama was taken aback. "Doing what – flapping his wings? Or is he a fisherman, is that what you're saying? Am I to be mother-in-law to a pirate? Or is it that he is simply shiftless? Shiftless is acceptable, assuming he's independently wealthy. *Is* he independently wealthy, Matilda? Please say yes."

Maddy, standing like a specimen in the centre of the room, felt as if her teeth and tongue and throat had all turned into glass. She tightened her fists, she would not bend. "Feather owns nothing, Mama. Only the clothes he wears."

Papa shook out his newspaper. "Sounds a sensible chap to me."

Maddy spun to him hopefully. "Papa, he is! You would like him—"

But it was just the iron man enjoying the game. "A man doesn't need material goods. They're bad for the willpower. A chap should provide himself with what he needs to be comfortable, and invest the remainder in bonds."

"Bonds!" Mama made a curt huffy noise. "Who cares what a man needs? A woman needs jewels. Does his mother wear diamonds, Matilda? Because diamonds are wonderful to inherit."

Maddy, embattled, finally twitched; she stamped her foot, and sand jumped from her shoe onto the fancy carpet. "He doesn't have bonds, and he doesn't have a mother! Feather's not rich! He's poor!"

Mama kept her serenity; only her mouth puckered with enjoyment. "Darling," she purred, "why love a pauper, when it's so easy to love a rich man? Forget this dustbin ragamuffin, Matilda. He's obviously after your money."

Maddy stared at her mother furiously, this woman like a redback spider, stylishly clad and venomous. "Why are you like this, Mama?" she asked. "Why is love worth so little to you?"

Her mother reared up, instantly freezing cold. "I'll teach you the cost of love," she snapped. "If you run off with some pauper then your father will cut you out of his will. Let's see what birdy boy thinks about *that*."

Maddy's black eyes went to her father, but it was the iron man who glanced over the newspaper at her. "I will not let a layabout get his hands on your inheritance, Matilda," he confirmed. "I've worked too hard to see it wasted by some fly-by-night."

Desperation thinned Maddy's blood and raised goosebumps on her arms. She crossed the room to kneel by her father's chair, and took his hand in her own. The iron man's palm was cool, but Maddy trusted that inside his skin there dwelt another man who was warm with kindness and affection for her. "Papa," she said, "Feather is my answer. Feather is my most beautiful thing. Have you forgotten the elephants and snowgeese we saw? The coral and fireflies? The most beautiful things in the world don't want money. I love Feather, Papa, and he loves me. I'd rather have nothing, than be without him. All I ask from you and Mama is that you be happy for us."

"Happy!" Mama gagged. "Happy to see I've raised a harebrain? This is all *your* fault." She turned hissing to Papa, waving her thin arms. "Filling the girl's head with poppycock about beauty – idiotic! It's time you grew up, Matilda, and understood a thing or two. The world is *not* a beautiful place. Everyone is out to snatch what they can, and they'll shove you into the dirt if you're in the way. You can't put faith in anything. Everything dies. The prettiest things are the first to decay. You're a fool if you think otherwise, Matilda, and your father is a fool for letting you. Tomorrow morning you're taking the first train out of this backwater, and you'll not come home until this absurdity is gone from your head!"

Maddy looked with alarm to her father, who merely eyed his wilful child, the inheritor of all that was leonine and good in him. She clutched his hand, Mama flamed her eyes, the ancestors craned forward on their hooks and wire, eager to hear what he'd say. When Papa eventually spoke, it was to say, "A man more beautiful than a sea-eagle? This is something I must see. Invite your Feather over for dinner next Sunday night."

"Absolutely not! *Absolutely not!*"

Maddy and Papa ignored Mama. Maddy hugged her father's hand. Another day, when there was time, she would tell him how much she loved him, how his presence in her heart eased her loneliness and made her strong. For now, there were more pressing things on her mind. Inviting Feather to the house would be like trying to coax a deer indoors, he would surely re-fuse; yet this opportunity could not be allowed to slip. "Come to the cove instead," she suggested. "You can meet him right now, today."

"Very well!" said her mother, startling even the ancestors. "Let us meet this feather-duster, this pigeon! Let us hear him sing! Matilda, bring my parasol!"

And while her mother was rigged in her hat, gloves and boots, and her father's hair was combed and his summer coat plucked of lint, Maddy sat on the couch in a deepening stew of regret, her heart descending to her knees. Until now Feather had been hers alone, in-describably perfect and precious. Sharing him would surely besmirch that pristine past, and fracture the peace of the future. As she followed her parents across the lawn and into the bushland Maddy was mute and reluc-tant, aware that every footstep was carrying her closer to disaster. Dabbling in Feather's clean life, exhibiting him like a curiosity: she was ruining everything. She stumbled along, prodded by twigs and leaves, swiping at the sticky flies, feeling hateful and sick. She dreaded to think what Feather would say when the three of them crowded onto his beach. Mama would crow to see him; Feather, seeing her, would recoil. He would never forgive Maddy for bringing them; they would never recover from being brought. With each moment that drew them nearer the cove, Maddy's worlds came closer to colliding. The nargun snarled and barked at her to change course. Birds dashed through the trees crying. Yet Maddy's mouth stayed stubbornly closed, her gaze fixed hard on the ground. What a flighty, fatuous little girl she would seem, if she were to change her mind now.

A cowardly piece of her began to wish that Feather was a dream even now dissolving.

Instead he was doing handstands by the water's edge. At the sight of Maddy and her parents he turned upright, and stared as if they were more peculiar than camels. His trousers appeared more than usually scrappy. His nose was peeling from sunburn. "Goodness, it's a savage," gasped Mama. "I think I'm going to faint."

But Maddy felt a surge of love for the queer smoky creature reflected in the shallows. He would never be angry or disappointed – he would forgive her anything, he would laugh and understand. She skittered across the sand to him, catching his brown fingers in her own. "Mama, Papa, this is Feather!" And instead of being sorry, she was outrageously proud.

Mama stood rigid on a sand dune. "If this is a joke, Matilda," she said, "it is in very poor taste."

But her father only stood and studied Feather, his thumbs hooked in his waistcoat, saying not a word.

Maddy knew he was thinking about their quest for beautiful things. Papa would see that Feather was like a fine brumby colt, something worth catching and owning. He removed his hat, inclined his head and said graciously, "How do you do, Mr Feather. I am Matilda's father. As her father, I do what I can to protect her, and to make her happy.

Sometimes these ambitions clash: sometimes, to protect her, I have to make her unhappy. But this afternoon it is me who is glum, because my daughter has informed me she is in love. As you can imagine, those are worrying words for a father to hear. Love has its drawbacks, as I'm sure you know. But I do want to see her happy, and there's happiness in her voice when she speaks of you. Maddy says she loves you, Mr Feather. What I would like to know is, do *you* love *her* in return?"

"This is not funny!" Mama screeched, scattering a distant herd of cows.

Papa and Maddy and Feather paid her no attention. Maddy looked at Feather, wringing his hand, her blood sounding louder than the waves thumping the shore. She knew he could crush her badly now, with just a shake of his head. He had never said the word *love*, as if it were something too heavy to pick up. If he disavowed her now, before Mama and Papa, there would be nothing left to do but return home and lock herself in her room, and lie down and seep away.

Feather's grey gaze left Papa's shrewd face, and travelled across the sand and up into the hills. From a nearby pillar of stone, a black-browed tern launched itself into the sky. It flew off quickly, calling stridently, its mission urgent. Maddy saw its wings shutter inside Feather's eyes. He bowed his fair head and she knew he saw everything: the harm he could do her, the cracks pulling through his world. In her mind she saw a wild thing, crouching and snared. Feather sighed softly, and looked up at Papa. "Yes, I love her. I do."

"No!" Mama bawled. "No, no!"

Maddy caught her breath, feeling she might cry. She bit her tongue against shouting the jubilance she felt. Papa was nodding, already making iron plans. "You live on a beach," he pointed out to Feather. "Clearly my daughter can't do the same. She is my most beautiful thing, and I want her to be properly cared for. You may think nothing of wind and hail, but Matilda is accustomed to crockery and doors. You are not the man I'd have chosen for my daughter, Mr Feather, though I am not surprised *she* has chosen *you*. For the sake of her happiness, I am prepared to com-promise – provided you do the same. Prove your love for her, sir, by quitting your undomesticated ways, and live life as a civilized fellow, as the rest of us do."

"But Papa," Maddy started, "the beach—"

"It is not negotiable, Matilda," said her father.

Maddy, wide-eyed, looked to Feather, whose

consideration had returned to the straggly hills. She knew someone better than herself would say *don't do it, Feather, don't agree*. But Maddy was herself, and she loved and wanted him, so she stood in anxious silence and said nothing and saved nothing, hungering for him to agree. And when, without turning his sights from the hills, Feather nodded and said, "I will," Maddy did not feel like the architect of a gaol, but exultant and victorious, and no longer alone.

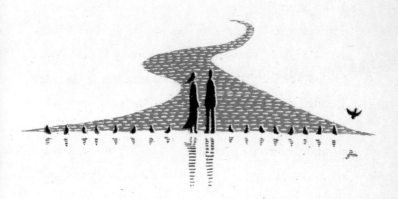

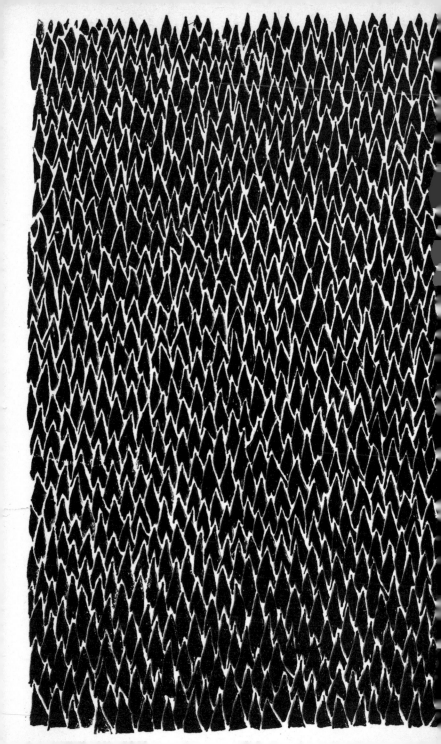

Because neither of them wanted to stroll in the park or hear the street sounds or drink iced tea with the neighbours, Maddy and Feather went to live in a quaint cottage in a forgotten field far from town, a place in which nobody had lived for many years. The house had four rooms and a falling-down fence, and its kitchen chimney was plugged by a possum's nest. A deep black forest of tall pine trees surrounded the cottage and its field, but on a sunny day the ocean could be seen in glittering glimpses between the spindly conifer branches. The overrun garden was jostling with flowers and weeds, and the field was flouncy with blue butterflies. Behind the house was a wide and depthless pond of enigmatic splashings. Maddy's mother turned ashen when she saw the cottage, and swore she would never come again. "I hope you're pleased, Matilda," she said, turning away with a twisting smile. Maddy's father laughed and laughed at the cottage, like a nasty boy giggling at a doll's house: but he could not deny that it had several doors and that its cupboards were full of crockery. "I am here if you need me," he told his daughter, yet Maddy needed nothing more. She was burrowed away from the world that perplexed her; she had Feather, and a forest to keep him secret; for company they had her little cat, Perseus; in such seclusion they would be safe. She slipped her arm through Feather's and said, "We will be happy here."

"If we must be anywhere," he answered, "I am glad we're here."

And it seemed to Maddy that no two people had, in fact, been happier. She filled the cottage with interesting things she had brought home from her travels, as well as stones and mouse skeletons and empty cocoons that she found on her rambles through the forest with Perseus. Feather pottered in the garden each day, gathering fallen rose leaves and brushing pine needles from the paths. Because the forest threw chill shadows on him, Maddy sewed him a wardrobe of clothes. She chose material that matched his storm-coloured eyes, adding buckles and buttons and many wide pockets in case he found something to carry. The rustling field was threaded with nettles, so she measured his feet and bought boots. He looked handsome as he drifted around the house, his throat and wrists bound by collars, his boots creaking like cellar doors. He looked different from the young man she had found on a beach with a pelican in his arms, the bronze fading out of his skin now, his hair darkened by the forest's shade. She loved to see him blinky-eyed at breakfast, or frowning at the thoughts in a book. She found herself wishing she had just one friend, to whom she might show him off.

She sat on the doorstep with Perseus in her lap and watched him work in the field, tilling the soil for vegetables, the grass flattening into paths under his boots. In the garden he rescued beetles from the birdbath, and scattered seeds and biscuits for the animals that visited the garden. He stopped and listened to subtle sounds of the forest, smiling in sympathy, cocking an ear. He

tasted raindrops and pine sap and pools of
mud, he watched the wind bend the
flimsy tips of the conifers.

He knelt in the ancient
flowerbeds, pulling dandelions and buttercups
from between shrubs. "What are you doing, Feather?"
Maddy asked, when she saw his scratched, smudged
hands.

He said, "I don't think a garden is supposed to
have weeds."

She stopped beside him, somehow unsure. She
had always rather admired weeds, being something of
a weed herself, eking out an existence, not expecting
much. After a moment of hesitation she said, "I don't
know why weeds are punished for being what they

are. Look at that one, squeezed into a crack – it's given no tending, but it never complains. Look at this one, clinging to stones – what flower could live fiercely as that? Weeds have roots and leaves and petals, the same as other plants. Why, then, should they be banished?"

Feather shrugged slackly. "I don't know. Isn't it how things are meant to be? Isn't a garden for jonquils, and lily-of-the-valley?"

And it was true that all the gardens Maddy had known were completely free of weeds. On their search for the world's most beautiful thing, she and her father had never stopped to admire dock or shepherd's purse. Feather could leave the weeds to thrive, she supposed, but then the garden might be ugly, not beautiful. Their house might seem laughable, their life together unconvincing. She wanted herself and Feather to be unassailable, for nothing to be wrong. "I'll help you," she said, turning back her sleeves.

After this, it seemed to Maddy that the cottage was not as nice or as proper as it could be. The windows and walls were grubby, the rooms smelled dimly of earth. She and Feather could not live like birds on the beach – but nor should they live like bears in a cave. They needed somewhere fitting to be. So she filled buckets and soaped surfaces until the glass and walls were spotless; she went to town and bought material to make curtains for the windows. She waited for the possum to venture out one night, then blocked up the chimney and burned the furry, flea-bitten bed. She oiled all the hinges that squawked, and gave the furniture refreshing coats of paint. She worked from morning until midnight, finding one thing after another in need of attention. Every well-finished chore made her feel more certain that theirs was a world that could last. One evening Feather came through the noiseless front door and, seeing his reflection in the

newly polished floor, stood still, peering down. "Do you like it?" Maddy asked. She herself was very pleased. Smoothing and polishing the timber had been the work of many days. "Take off your boots," she told him. "I don't want you to ruin it."

Feather glanced at his boots, which were heavy and stiff as horseshoes and rubbed the skin from the back of his heels. "I like floors when they are still trees," he said. "I like sunshine on water more than polish from a jar."

"So do I!" Maddy said quickly. "I like those things too!"

Feather did not answer, but stared at his reflection. As if talking to somebody unseen, he explained, "This is how things are meant to be."

A blade of unease cut into Maddy's satisfaction. "You look tired," she said, because she didn't know what else to do.

And in fact they often were tired, and sometimes grumpy for it. The days of sitting together idly watching the waves were a long time in the past. Before there'd been leaks to plug and garments to mend, they'd had nothing to do but linger and talk. Now they toiled and slept, and not much more. They no longer searched for faces in the clouds, or walked through the forest at midnight. They spoke a lot about the house, and hardly ever about the people who lived in it. Maddy stopped confiding in the nargun, because she had no time for anything that wasn't necessary and real. Perseus would run when he heard the approach of her bustling feet. Feather learned to wield an axe against a sapling for the fire or a rooster for the dinner table. Seeing him in his boots and trousers, his white shirt and leather belt, it was difficult to imagine that he'd once lived by the ocean like a sea-bird or a seal. Clothed and preoccupied, the strange smoky shimmer that swam from him was scarcely noticeable any more. Maddy still called him Feather, but it was easy to forget why.

Autumn passed, then winter. And eventually there came a day when all the weeds were pulled from the garden, and roses grew instead; when the fetid water had been drained from the pond, and clear water rippled there; when the garden paths curved in tidy lines, without a pine needle in sight; when the picket fence had been nailed, and stood militarily straight. The windows of the cottage were curtained, the floors were marzipan-smooth. The quilts were sewn, the chimneys swept, the holes in the walls were patched. Everything was finally proper, and there was nothing now for Feather and Maddy to do except live. Standing in the shadow of their perfect house, he asked, "Are you happy?"

"I am," said Maddy. For how could she not be? She curled her hand in his. "Are *you* happy, Feather?" she asked. "I hope so."

Because she had not forgotten the grave sacrifices he had made for her, the things he'd bravely fare-welled; and it did not matter what she felt, as long as he was content.

He said, "I am happy that you are."

But one day she could not find him, and after searching the field and then the forest she found him a long long walk away, sitting on the beach. The sight of him alone on the sand, his knees drawn up, his face turned to the breeze, had once filled Maddy with soaring delight. Now it chilled her to the core. She rushed down the sand and fluttered around him, saying, "Come home, it's getting late, you can't stay out all night." Yet her dismayed heart knew very well that he *could*, if he wanted to – Feather could stay out all night, all day, forever. He was not afraid of the dark. When Maddy first met him, before he'd been given a key and a door, the clouds and earth had been Feather's roof and floor, his companions and home. It was a relief when he stood, pulled on his boots, and returned to the cottage with her. He slept soundly that night, his lovely head on plump pillows; but Maddy lay awake watching the spiny shadows of trees quavering in the wind.

From that day onward, whenever Feather slipped from sight, fear jabbed Maddy like a rusty nail. She would skitter from room to room, calling him. She'd discover him kneeling in the vegetable patch or digging rocks from the field. Hearing panic in her voice, he would look up with confusion. Embarrassed, Maddy would try to pretend she wasn't worried about anything at all. One day, however, Feather understood – he overheard the whisper that was telling her terrible things. He bent his head to hers and said, "Look, Maddy, I'm here."

But another morning, soon after, she found him once more by the ocean. He was standing barefoot on the rocks and looking out to sea. There was surely something out there – Maddy couldn't see it, but she knew that Feather could. Inside himself, he saw something to which she was blind. He looked at it more devoutly than he ever looked at her. Of all the things that were important to him, this thing was immortal.

He reached for his boots when he saw her, slipped them on his feet. "I'm here," he said again.

Some nights, reading by the fire, she would glance up to see him staring down at his empty hands. Some days, watching through the kitchen window, she saw him gaze searchingly into the sky. He was listening, thinking, remembering: she realized he was pining. She wanted to run outside and strike him, because he was hurting her. It wasn't right – he shouldn't want to hurt her, he wasn't *allowed* to cause her pain, not when he knew that she loved him, not when she strove so hard to be loved. She said, "You have a life with me now, you're happy," in case he didn't know.

And then one morning, one terrible day, she found him walking by the water without his boots and shirt, as unkempt as any creature who'd never been inside a house. He looked as wild as he had on the day she'd first met him – Maddy thought she saw a flare of lightning flicker in his wake. Worse than this, though, was the troop of gulls that trotted alongside him. The birds stepped smartly, like busy little barristers, tense chatter rising between them. The flock of birds and the unclothed, unshackled man strode down the beach, full of purpose and determination. There was clearly something important that they needed to do.

Maddy stepped back among the conifers before she was seen, dizzy with exile. There were things in Feather's life that he shared, but not with her.

Wandering aimlessly from tree to tree, she realized that he would never tell her what he saw when he looked to sea. This thing belonged to him, it was private and important, and he wouldn't tell her what it was because he was not obliged. "Feather isn't yours." The nargun put it succinctly, appearing unbidden by her side. "And you are less important than this mysterious, summoning thing. And whatever it is, its summons is loud. Loud enough to carry him away from you. What shall you do? What shall you do?"

That night at supper Maddy said, "I don't like the forest. It is too dark. Let's go to the desert, where there are no trees or ocean, just the sun over our heads."

Feather nodded and said mildly, "If that will make you happy."

"Won't it make you unhappy?"

Feather said, "It will make no difference to me."

And that was how he told her it didn't matter where they lived – by the coast, in a canyon, on the top of a hill; in a cottage, in a chamber, in a box underground. In his heart, he would always be looking elsewhere. A sea-bird only cares for wind and water and sky: starved, blind, fallen to earth, its thoughts still turn to flight.

His words blurred Maddy's vision, made her feel threadbare and fraught. She couldn't bear losing him to this shapeless need. She would fight to keep him – but how to battle something that has less substance than air? And if she fought it, and if it died, wouldn't part of Feather die too? In misery she pleaded, "Tell me, Feather. I'd like to know. Let me take some of the burden from you. Explain it to me."

"I can't," he replied, quite simply.

Her shoulders fell, she knotted her fingers. "We *can* be happy, Feather. You *can* be, if you try."

Like a weary doll he answered, "I am happy, Maddy. You don't think I love you, but I do."

They sat together at the table in sorrow, the lonely fairytale princess and the wondrous being chained to the ground.

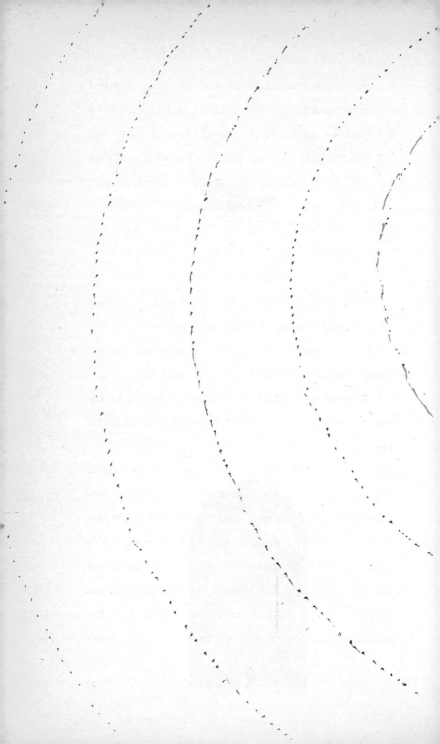

There was no one to whom Maddy could describe her woe: they never had any visitors, and she had no friends who weren't make-believe or feline. Her mother would only laugh deliciously, as a kind of revenge. She could not tell her adventurous father, because he would be pained, and believe that her troubles were a fault of his own. The iron man, always quick to criticize, would be loud in his contempt of Feather. In the iron man's world, a healthy young fellow did not spend his days staring moonily out to sea. So Maddy kept her unhappiness a secret to herself. She didn't want Feather blamed and hounded just for being who he was. And yet, if he were different, things would not be so bad. Everything would be blissful, Maddy believed, if only Feather could forget who he was.

He walked around the garden as if the pickets were a row of steel bars. He dug the soil and cleaned the birdbath and swept leaves from the door. The sight of him dutifully filling his days made Maddy feel sunken and hollow. She remembered the zoos she had visited on her hunt for beauty – the wolves pacing stone, the waxen starfish behind glass. The animals had been netted from jungles and plains, the sea creatures scooped from the waves. Somehow, they had all been cornered and trapped. Maddy had her own beautiful thing now, something *she* had cornered and trapped. She should have left him alone, maybe; she certainly had no right to resent his restlessness. But she longed for him to be happy, to be hers: so she would not open the prison of her heart to let him go. "I love you," she told him, and this was true, and she knew that he believed her; but when she said it she saw the chain around his ankle, a length of links that let him wander, but not far. She did not see the chain around her own ankle, because love is blind.

He went down to the beach most mornings, and

she did not run to find him. Sometimes he disappeared at dawn and did not return until dark. She thought about the day a bird had brought to him a sardine in its curved beak. On evenings when Feather didn't come home for supper, Maddy supposed he was dining with petrels and cormorants. Once, the thought would have been magical. Now it made her feel lost.

She tried to make things different. She tried to make herself shiny in his mind. She was always laughing. She never complained about the afternoons she spent alone while he gazed at the sea. She tried not to ask too many questions or to say things she'd said before. She hoped that, if she were vibrant enough, he would forget his distractions and come to her. The plan did not seem to work. She felt like a ship buoyantly riding the waves while, under water, its hull is splintering on the reef. Feather laughed with her, and slept by her side, and saw she was vibrant and smiled to see it, and looked away.

Together they were two cheerful souls racked by melancholy. Maddy kept herself alive: she read, she learned to cook, she played with Perseus and a ball of wool, she walked among the conifers. But she was living like a puppet, whose heart is merely wood.

Then one afternoon, while she was mashing potatoes, Maddy felt a tremble – the same small tremble a river must feel when a leaf drops onto its surface and sends ripples to the distant banks. She stood still, her thoughts inside herself, and in an instant felt it again – the flick of a sparrow's wing. She put down the masher, astonished. Her mind was bare: but her world woke up, shook itself, and stepped out into the light.

She looked at the ceiling, and around at the room. She saw nothing ordinary, not a saucepan, not a chair, nothing she had seen a thousand times before, but only things startling and incredible. Without even trying, something miraculous had happened, and everything was different after all. She ran all the way to the beach, her skirts streaming behind her, fancying she could run forever, that she could leap higher than a tree. The tide was coming in, and Feather was investigating puddles for sea-bugs stranded by the waves. When he heard her calling he looked up warily, as if he might fly. Maddy took his hand and pressed it to her. She was puffing so hard she could hardly speak. "Feel," she said.

102

His hand left a damp print on her dress. She saw him understanding, a smoky kindling in his eyes. "A nymph," he said. "A little elf. A tiny fay."

"Ours," she said, and hugged him, and flopped into the sand, grinning at the sky. The syrupy orange sunlight pooled in her palms and poured out between her fingers. She and Feather had coasted far from each other: but this fay was a link, a grace, a clear light. It would be the best of them – them dauntless and to-gether. The fay meant it wasn't cruel to love Feather, for nothing so wonderful could come from something wrong. For the first time in a long time, Maddy was happy when she laughed.

Matilda smiled down at her lined hands, squinting as if the beachside sun still tilted in her eyes. "How brilliant everything seemed at that moment," she said. "How promising. I thought that, finally, I could bring Feather joy. I thought that finally, after all I'd taken from him, I could give something back."

The boy was sitting cross-legged on the carpet, stroking Peake's head. The flames of the heater were casting a red hue on his chin and nose. "Are you hungry?" Matilda asked, suddenly remembering her manners. "I'll make you some supper. There is soup and sausages, and some peaches for dessert."

"I'm not hungry," said her guest, although it was a boy's dinner time. "Maybe later. I don't like peaches."

"Well, you needn't have them. I don't want to make you miserable."

The boy nodded, not interested. With one hand he smoothed down the dog's peppy ears, which instantly popped up again. Without looking at her, he asked, "So did it happen like you wanted – did everything change that day?"

Matilda paused, unsure what to say. She did not know how far a child should be invited into the world of his elders. With its hard laws and complicated outcomes, the grown-up world was not a good place for children. Yet she wanted to say aloud this thing she had kept under a dark cloak for endless years: she needed to speak it, and see it, and test how much it still hurt. And the boy was waiting, his fingers gliding over the dog.

"Lying on the beach that afternoon," she began carefully, "I really believed the fay would give Feather reason to look away from the horizon. Reason to change himself, although I did not want him to change. How doltish love and loneliness can be, some-times. I thought that, because the fay filled me with joy, it would do the same for Feather. I must not have understood anything about him – or even about life, for life doesn't work that way. I learned this that very day, when I stood up to leave. I brushed the sand from my dress, and held out my hand to Feather. But he shook his head and told me that he wished to sit a while longer on the beach, alone. I could go, he said. But he preferred to stay."

Dismissed, she had walked home in a kind of dumb shock, her arms lank by her sides, the gleam of the fay dulled. In her mind hulked a truth like a mas-sive, rusty, untolling bell. *Nothing* – nothing she did, nothing she could do, nothing built or invented, no one born or unborn – could make Feather turn away from his horizon.

The boy made no comment, but kept his eyes on Peake, his teeth pushed into his lip.

"At first," she said, "I could hardly bear to look at Feather. I wanted to scratch him, to wound him, to cause him some kind of illness. Around me hung a fog of shame, as if I were guilty of a crime. I told myself he was an unfeeling and heartless man ... but I never believed what I said. Feather was not a bad man. He was a kestrel, an eel, a lacewing. He begrudged nothing else its life, but *his* life belonged absolutely to him. This is how wild things are. This is what I had loved about him in the first place. And that is why I forgave him. That is what kept me loving him."

Expecting protests, Matilda glanced over her glasses; but the boy ignored this mention of his least-favourite sentiment and tickled Peake under the chin, echoing in a pleased humming voice, "A kestrel. An eel."

Matilda smiled at him, and looked aside; when she spoke again, it was mostly to herself. "As the days passed, I saw there was no sense in regretting the way things were. Instead, I began to think of how they might be. Feather, I decided, could have the great heaving ocean: the miniscule fay was something for me. Feather wanted whatever it was he sought on the horizon: I wanted the fay. It would be ours, but it would really be mine. As soon as I decided this, I began thinking about the fay all the time. It was a kite in my mind, high above every thought. I gave it a thousand different names, trying to find the right note. I couldn't help wondering what it would look like – fair and willowy, or dark like me? I hoped it could be both, like a lark's tail. At night I lay awake brooding on all the things I needed to know. There was so much I would have to teach it. I knew mathematics and geography and the correct way to address a queen, I knew how to follow an animal's tracks and how wagtails build their round nests, but there were a thousand simple things that were inexplicable to me. How could I teach it to be wise? How could I save it from making mistakes? What are the instructions for living an honourable life? I was often doubtful, and sometimes afraid – but mostly I was blithesome. Nothing was made right, because of the fay: but everything ceased to be awry. Nothing was sour or spoiled any more. Now, when Feather was gone, I talked to the fay. And it listened to me, I believed – it fluttered and spun and swirled. I dreamed of how its voice would sound, of what its first words would be. I wondered if it would like me, if it would like the cottage and the forest and field. I secretly worried that it would prefer the beach – that it, too, would spend its days tramping the shore like a poor creature in a cell. But I didn't really believe that: I knew the fay was mine. I saw us sitting under trees, I saw it asleep in my arms. I felt the beating of its blood, the tenderness of its skin. I think I fell in love with it, that tiny, invisible thing."

The boy didn't look up from stroking the dog; he asked, "Did you love it more than you loved Feather?"

"Feather was beautiful," Matilda said, "and I really did love him. But the fay would have been the most beloved thing in the world."

But then, one day, the little fay stopped spinning. Maddy was threading blue stalks of lavender into a vase when the ripples inside her broke on the river bank, and faded into stillness. Limp stems of lavender fell from her hands, water spilled from the vase to the floor. Maddy dived frantically into herself as the fay sunk soundlessly down. In the blackness, she couldn't see it. In the slick grief already pouring from her heart, she couldn't catch the tiny gold body. "No," she cried, "no, no—" but the little fay was dying, was already dead. Its flimsy winged body wafted over and over, and soon disappeared in the dark.

Feather, of course, was nowhere to be found. Maddy stretched out on the cool floor, her face pressed to the polished wood. The tears that slipped down her cheeks made a puddle under her. With deadly silence, despair tore through the ground, ripping open a depthless crevasse. She looked into this ruined world and saw nothing but grit and shattered rubble. She could not speak, or draw breath. The walls, the table, the ceiling thinned. The flowers strewn about her wilted from purple to grey. Her agony was a rope tied around her neck. Maddy knew the pain would drown her.

She climbed to her feet, straightened her dress, and walked out into the garden. It was a clear sunny day, and bees were bumbling on the air. Birds called each other from tree tops, the cat was sleeping on the grass, and far away a young fox barked foolhardily. The sun kept shining, the breeze kept blowing, the earth kept turning round: only she had stopped.

Maddy walked along the path in naked brown feet, to the end of the garden where reeds grew and dragonflies sailed. Then she picked up the biggest rock she could carry, and leapt into the pond.

Down through the freezing water she went, the rock her greatest friend, plunging like a hound dashing after a scent, racing for the bottom. She closed her eyes and let the water streak past, raking back her long loosed hair, hauling at her sleeves. Its blackness and gaunt coldness made her think of the unseen side of the moon. Weeds swiped her face like ghostly hands wiping away laughter and tears. She felt the rock thud into the muddy bottom of the pond and knew all she had to do was hold on.

She kept her eyes closed, cradling the rock, and let the water find her. She could follow the fay easily if she merely waited and was brave. If she stayed here, in the arms of the pond, she would never again have to find her way to the end of another lonely day.

And then something warm and living touched her lips: startled, Maddy opened her eyes. Through the murk and knotty weeds she glimpsed a seal's sleek skin, the arrowheads of a wing. Feather scooped her to him and kicked strongly for the sky. They broke the dark surface trailing cat tails of clammy slime, gasping with the cold.

He dragged her spluttering from the water, and lay her on the grass. Maddy would never forget the feeling of crisp lawn at her shoulders, the leaden weight of her waterlogged dress. She lay limply, blinking at the sky, understanding that its blueness was a threat and a promise. No matter how wretched her life became, the sun would rise, the sky would glow. Everything was here for her, but none of it needed her. She sank in the grass, soaked and trembling, while all about her continued the beautiful world she no longer trusted and would not forgive.

"The fay is gone," she told Feather.

"I am sorry for your loss," he said.

Maddy did not even flinch. She looked at the sky, at the coasting clouds. Her thoughts were ice floating on a flat sea. She didn't look at Feather when she spoke, but she was thinking of him. "I will know, now, how it feels to long for something you don't have."

Feather said nothing. He pulled a shard of grass from the earth, and looked away. The shadow of the forest brushed the lawn, a blackbird plucked a rattling beetle from the air. In a voice terse with hopelessness he said, "None of this is what I wanted. None of it is the way it should be."

He stopped, and sighed, and wiped his eyes. Maddy felt sparer than air.

He picked her up and carried her inside, took off her wet clothes and put her gently into bed. He lay down beside her, and after a time she slept. When she woke, it was night, and where Feather had been the cat now lay ranged, its lime eyes regarding her peaceably. The sheets were undented, tucked up to the pillows. Maddy knew that this was her room now, that she would never sleep beside Feather again. She curled around herself, staring into the dark. Already her heart had begun its life-long mourning for her fay. She would learn to live with this, sometimes to even forget it: but it would stay with her forever, like a bad deed or a scar, a gnarled thing she could hardly ever bear to contemplate.

It wasn't until much later that it occurred to Maddy to wonder if Feather had dived into the pond to rescue her that day – or if he'd been there already, swimming alone, drifting in the unlit depths.

The seasons make no difference to pine trees. In autumn they keep their swarthy needles as the days shorten and the sunshine weakens. Winter, with its livid clouds and squalls, suits the draughty gloom of the pine trees' darkness, their majestic austerity. Their thick white roots impoverish and harden the soil, so only the toughest weeds may take hold. In spring when the grasslands surrounding the pines are speckled with bright wildflowers, the forest remains craggy and colourless but for red-capped toadstools, sepsis-yellow fungus. No animal eats the acrid needles, so apart from

113

wasps in their high, thrumming nests, nothing makes its home in the branches. No Dreamtime creature prowls the shadows, no sprite skitters, no thylacine sniffs from tree to tree. Nothing is born or hunted here. The conifer forest is alive, and yet it is not. It is an unaltering landscape, a live painting. It is a living thing that doesn't draw breath.

One day, a day like any other, marked a year since Maddy and Feather had come to live in the cottage behind the picket fence, in the pine forest's sharp-smelling shade.

Maddy made a cake to mark the occasion, and invited Feather to share it with her at his favourite place, the beach. He lifted his head, smiling uncertainly. "A picnic?"

"Yes, why not? We'll bring a blanket to sit on, and some sarsaparilla."

"I've never been on a picnic," Feather said. "We should have had a picnic every day."

Maddy imagined the two of them dining like foxes in the forest. Throughout the warm and windless days since Feather had hauled her from the pond, bulbs had sprouted, the roses had bloomed, pollen had powdered the air. A new generation of birds had been hatched and taught to fly. The nights were clear and frostless, the afternoons balmy and long. Everything in nature had filled the days swooning voluptuously into the arms of life. But through all this time Maddy and Feather had lived as quietly as foxes live, huddling up in their separate darknesses as foxes do. They had been kind to one another, they had held each other's hand – but each had used their empty hand to nurse their yearning heart. They talked to one another, but never about important things – never about a lost winged dream, not about unseeable mysteries that lay beyond the setting sun. They both knew that you can talk and talk, but when the talk is done and there's nothing else to say, the thing that you long for is still not there.

Sometimes Maddy felt they were both very old – older than the trees that barricaded them, older than the planet. Sometimes she felt they were two ancient creatures who had tumbled from the stars and who'd learned to live where they had landed as well as they could.

It was a still, mauve evening, and the tide had brought the ocean high up the sand. Oystercatchers veered over the shallows while silver gulls stood around on one leg. The green water was choppy, like a bicycle ride on a rough path, sloshing over the pitted rocks and fetching up sticks like a dog. The sunset was coloured mango-pink and red; the sand was marbled and pale.

Feather spread the blanket in the shelter of an over-hang, and he and Maddy sat down. After the terrible day of the pond, Maddy had been ill for many weeks. She had wept and wept for the perished fay, had felt she would go mad with pity for the poor lost thing. She had found little to say to Feather, to whom the fay was a nothing returned to nothingness. But it was Feather who had tended and soothed her, and challenged her to live: and eventually Maddy had listened, though not before grief had made her thin and sunken-eyed, and chilled by the slightest gust of cold. She tightened her shawl around her shoulders, and looked about at the water and grainy cliffs the way she looked at everything now – as if she'd never before encountered such things, and wasn't sure what to make of them. She saw that the sea-birds were watching Feather, and that for her sake he was disregarding them. He cut wedges from the cake and toppled the slices onto plates. Maddy poured the sarsaparilla and they sat together in convivial silence, their elbows occasionally touching, enjoying their sweet-toothed feast. In silence they watched a dun crab struggling over the fringe of the blanket, and chuckled when a tiny white gnat skated the surface of Feather's drink. The gulls observed them intently from afar, swallowing their greed. Feather finished his piece of cake, and cut himself another. Maddy shaded her eyes and searched the horizon for a raft or bobbing wreckage, for a tidal wave. As always, she saw only an immense panorama of restive emptiness, blue as a kingfisher's mantle, forbidding as a wasteland. Distantly she wondered if Feather thought of the ocean as his enemy or his friend. She turned to him and asked, "Do you remember the day I found you on the beach with the pelican?"

Feather nodded, sucking pink icing from his thumb.

"Why were you there?" It was something she had never thought about before. "Had a sea-eagle dropped you from the sky?"

"I was there to meet you," he said, with a smile and the flicker of an eyebrow. "Somebody who knew what pelicans talk about." His words made Maddy smile shyly, although she didn't believe him. Since the day by the pond Feather was always saying pretty things that were like bubbles of air, things she doubted and brushed away. His face darkened, however, and he said, "I should not have stayed. When I first met you, you had no cares. You shone with all the fabulous things you had seen, your world was wide and full of colours. Now there are shadows under your eyes, and you live in a lonely forest."

"But I wanted you to stay." She was willing to take the blame. "I trapped you into being with me, and threw away the key."

Feather shook his fair head. "That's silly, Maddy. There never was a trap, there never was a key. I stayed because I wanted to. How else could I have shown you that I loved you?"

Her heart was wrung by those thistle-down words, which floated off lighter than air. "We should leave this place, Feather," she said – and only when she'd said it did Maddy realize how much she wanted and meant it, how determined she felt. "Let's go to the place that will make you happy, and then I can be happy too—"

"No." He laid a hand against her face, quietening her. "You can't come with me."

She stared at him, at his fine ashy eyes, his long straight eyelashes, the strangeness that haloed him. She understood. She knew he had made sacrifices; she'd known they would prove unendurable; she knew he would fly eventually. Even so, a fragment of her had always insisted on hoping she was mistaken. Now that fragment broke, and blew away, and there was no dignity in chasing after it, or in arguing. Maddy had done what she could to keep and console him; she had tried to be forgivable, and she had forgiven. Nothing had been enough. She gazed across the ocean and asked, "What should I have done?"

"Nothing." Feather smiled. "I love you, Maddy, and I always will. I will never forget you. But I have to go. There's somewhere else I need to be – someone else I have to be. Every day that I am not those things, a light goes out in me."

She could only stare numbly at the water – she couldn't think what to say. She watched the turgid turning of the deep waves, heard the ceaseless sigh of the tide. She searched for a light inside herself, but she couldn't remember what light looked like, or how it felt. Feather didn't know that he was, in fact, fortunate. She said, "I suppose I should be grateful that you've stayed as long as you have."

"I have been happy here," Feather said firmly. "Never think it's been any other way."

They sat side-by-side, no longer touching, watching the sun fuse liquidly into the horizon. A gull, unable to resist further temptation, quick-stepped to the edge of the blanket, its scarlet eyes fixed on Feather. He filled his palms with cake crumbs, and the bird speedily pecked them clean. Then it lifted its wings to the breeze and flew away over the water.

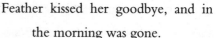

They walked home together, and Feather tried to be merry and to act as if nothing was different. Maddy went to bed and lay awake listening to the whiskery sough of the forest. Some time during the night Feather kissed her goodbye, and in the morning was gone.

The boy in the lounge room asked, "Gone where?"

Matilda looked away from the beach and the seagull, the slices of cake on plates. "Who knew?" She meant to sound chirpy. "He had arrived from nowhere, and I assumed he went back there. In the morning, I didn't even search for him. I knew I wouldn't find a clue. He left nothing behind, except everything. His clothes were neatly folded, his boots were by the door. Feather was finished with that part of his life – the forest, the cottage, his garden. The failed promise, the fay.

121

And me. We had all been put into his past."

The boy pinched his lip, thinking on this. Matilda saw that he couldn't decide what was wrong and what was right. "What did you do?" he asked.

She smiled ruefully, closing her eyes. She was tired – in the pit of her bones, she was actually exhausted. So many years had passed between the picnic on the purple beach and this gloamy late-afternoon: she felt she should pack a case and rug up warmly before remembering back so far. Peake was lying on his mat, paws quivering as he dreamed. Matilda felt oddly tempted to lie down beside him, to feel the carpet like grass against her cheek. "For such a long time," she told the boy, "I did nothing. I lived like an old crone – or maybe like a fairytale princess who's been cursed. Everything was motionless, a river that's stopped flowing. Every morning I made breakfast for Perseus and myself, which we ate in a patch of sun. During the day I worked in the garden, growing vegetables and picking the fruit. I made sandwiches for lunch, and cut them into squares. I swept the floors and washed the pots, I picked stones from the soles of my shoes. There were many things to do. At night I drew the curtains and dozed with the cat on my lap, listened to the wind. Sometimes, even though I held them close to the fire, my hands felt cold as earth. I thought about Feather, the things he had said, the sound of him laughing, the smell of him. I thought, too, of the fay, about the life I would be living if the fay had stayed with me. At night I dreamed about them, and woke up feeling drained. In this huge world, I had only wanted two things, and they'd both slipped beyond my reach. I walked through the forest with my eyes on the ground, as if I might find something I'd once dropped without realizing, something that would explain. I thought about how long people live – so many days to stand up in, so many nights to watch through. I thought of all the errors you can make in a lifetime, the decisions you may make once and never again. After a few weeks, I stopped thinking about anything – it's easily done. If the only things you have to think about are things that hurt you, your mind has mercy, and builds a white box, and lets you hide inside."

And despite the years that had shouldered past since then, Matilda remembered clearly how it had been, those weeks and weeks inside a thoughtless box, whose walls were glacial, whose ceiling dripped snow.

A puppet, she'd been made of wood, which could be whittled away. Every move she made was unwilling, something she had no heart to do. Her eyes, her smile, the blush of her skin: all these were painted on. No part of her felt like a real self – she was only strings and jointed limbs. She had loved hugely, and lost what she'd loved. This was damage that could never fully repair. From now on, she would always be someone who could be lifted up, danced about, dropped aside, and hurt.

She'd wanted only to lie down and let lonesomeness and disappointment settle around her like ravens. She hadn't understood why her body strove to stay above ground, when her spirit so craved the dark.

Matilda opened her eyes abruptly, and blinked several times at the boy. "Forgive me for telling you this," she said. "It's probably quite boring to you."

The boy, sprawled like a retriever on the settee, replied with a slight grimace, acknowledging that, though hardly enthralled, he would endure. His honesty revived Matilda, who looked at he self, at her hands with their spots and rumples, at her old feet in their sensible shoes, and said, "It's hard to believe this wrinkled body is the same one I lived in back then. Then I was young, and my skin fit snugly. I didn't have lines, my hair wasn't grey, I did not smell of cold porridge. My mind, too, was youthful. Maybe an elderly mind could live in a white box, and find it tranquil. But I was young, and my mind was bruised, but it was still sprightly. Like a toddler in church, it couldn't stay quiet. It began to hunt for a way out. Like a toddler, it started to piece together words. It asked questions which felt like a nip. *If he loved me, why did he leave? If he loved me, why am I alone?*"

Matilda sat back, tapping her heel. "I didn't know much in those days," she said. "I was just a girl. I'd always imagined that love was something which couldn't be destroyed. I thought that, once conjured, love was towering and eternal. But wandering around the cottage alone, I began to suspect I was wrong. Maybe love was really a feeble, spineless thing, which easily forgets the thing it once adored. If that was true of ordinary love, then my love was different. My love was something colossal, my love was *great*. I wanted to stop loving Feather, but I simply could not. He had hurt me, he had deserted me, he had never tried – and he'd never wanted the fay. If Feather had ever loved me, it was only with that faulty, insipid love. And yet, despite all this, I missed him, and I longed for him to return.

125

I was shackled with love, I was blighted by it; I was its victim, plagued to despair. But Feather, I imagined, was carefree somewhere, never giving me a thought. He'd got everything he wished for, and nothing he didn't want. Me, though – I had nothing! A broken heart, that was all! And it wasn't fair – it made me angry – eventually, it made me kick and punch and smash my way out of that awful white box."

Her visitor looked up, pleased to hear violent words. The old lady's eyes were twinkling. "In those days," she told him, "I could be quite bad-tempered. In a wink, the dejection that paralysed me was booted out, and into its place sprang a fanged little sense of indignation. I threw aside my sandwich and stood up. I didn't want to live that way any more – falling and falling, waiting only to hit the ground. There was a question I needed to ask Feather – I'd been trying to think of the answer, but I couldn't work it out. For me, it was impossible. But Feather *must* know the answer, and I decided he was going to tell me."

Her guest showed his teeth. "What did you do?"

"I put on my hat, and rode my bicycle into town. I went down to the harbour, where the boat builder had his shed. I explained to the builder what I wanted:

a small lean boat with two tall sails, fast and able to travel far. The boat builder said he could do it, but that he would need time. Fortunately, I needed time too. I didn't know how to sail. But I paid a mean old sailor to teach me, and by the time my boat was launched I could handle a craft and navigate the water as easily as I could walk. I christened my boat the *Albatross*, because the air and the ocean love that bird, and she loves them in return. There was a man taking photographs of families on the pier, and I gave him a few coins to take a picture of me and my boat. I spent a week sailing her back and forth along the coast until we understood each other well."

Matilda's visitor smiled appreciatively; Matilda smiled too. It was good to be out on the open sea, far from the cottage and the forest.

"I packed the hold of the *Albatross* with as much food and water as the boat could carry. I bought a lamp, for sailing at night, and a pistol in case I met pirates. The evening before I sailed, I carried Perseus home to my father's house, because he was a land-loving cat. I'd intended to tell my parents of my plans, but at the dining table I changed my mind. For so long I had kept my thoughts to myself, it had become my habit. Telling them anything, at this far-gone moment, would only have spooked up a stampede of fuss. Besides: whether you're a child or an adult, there are things your parents never need to know. And throughout your whole life, there are things you must do without help or advice, things you can only do by yourself. I felt stronger and kinder, keeping my plans unexplained. Yet maybe Papa suspected something: as I was leaving, he embraced me and said, *Do as you must, but do so with care. Don't forget that I am here.*"

Matilda paused, taking off her glasses to rub her eyes. She had not wanted to step away from her father's shadow that evening. She had wanted to bury her face into his chest and ask him why he had left her over and over, abandoning her to the coldness of the iron man and her mother. But that was just a fool's question, and she had let it go, hurrying down the stairs without looking back. "I wish Papa were here now," she said, slipping her glasses on, and glancing at the boy. "I think you would like one another."

She left her parents' house early that night, and walked through the darkened scrub to the sea. On the beach where she had first met Feather, Maddy picked up a stick and scratched her impossible question into the sand. She stood back and waited under the milky moon and stars, watching the water wash up the beach and wave after wave take the letters away. She would search the planet until she found Feather, and when she did she would ask him the question, and then she would shake him until the answer fell out. It was the least that he owed her.

She set sail at sunrise, unaccompanied and unafraid. The sea breeze filled the ivory sails of the *Albatross* and blew Maddy's hair roguishly. She was setting out to circle the world again, but this time she was in search of just one beautiful thing. She imagined the answer as a link made of starlight, the most valuable treasure ever buried. It was her birthday, a good day to begin.

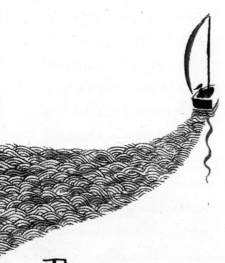

The *Albatross* skimmed the water like a dragonfly. Maddy sat by the tiller, keeping the boat's nose pointed at the horizon. Feather had looked with such longing at that line where the sky and the ocean meet as cleanly as do squares on a chess board, and Maddy kept her eyes on it too. She knew, of course, that the horizon is an unreachable thing – that the closer you get, the further away it glides – but she was undeterred. The question smouldered in her, demanding to be satisfied. She kept the rudder straight and the halyard ropes tight and the white sails angled to the wind, and the

Albatross sped across the waves as swiftly as a dart. The sea was green beneath her, and in its emerald depths Maddy glimpsed a landscape of seaweed and shoals of elegant fish. A seahorse raised its pointy snout as the shadow of the boat dashed past. When she next looked behind her, the land was far away. The town was made of tiny white pebbles, the scrub was a smeared blue haze. She imagined the nargun standing on a high hill, staring red-eyed after her. The nargun had been no consolation to her over the past terrible months, and it could not help her now. Maddy watched while the land grew thinner and thinner and finally disappeared. In every direction, then, she could see only water. It pleased her.

A boat is a simple thing, but in sailing there's much to do. The swell must be studied, the currents considered, the sails swung into the wind. Ropes must be tied and untied, the anchor wants dropping and lugging. Water needs bucketing from the vessel when waves splash over the side, and endless effort must be put into keeping everything dry. The ocean and sky demand vigilant study, for both can be prankish, and unexpectedly enraged. Maddy had no intention of letting her boat sink. In their days and nights traversing the ocean, she would become something more than pleased with the vessel: the *Albatross* became her best friend. She cared for it, willed her heart into it. She patched small holes in the canvas, and inspected the planks and caulking each dawn. In the long hours between midday and dusk she talked to the boat, understanding it and encouraging it. One day, when a black shadow cruised ominously beneath the keel, she stood up and shouted, "Shoo! Shoo!" And it wasn't so much for her own health she feared, as for the health of her boat.

Very quickly they left the green water behind. The deep ocean is a dark thing, though its waves are hemmed with wedding-lace foam and it twinkles beneath the sun. For most of the time, the scenery is the same. Above Maddy, the clouds morphed and shifted, but always remained clouds. The water chipped and chopped and yawned, but always stayed infinite. She saw no other boats, though she scanned the distance ceaselessly. Wherever her journey was taking her, it was to somewhere no one else was sailing to, nor returning from. Such solitude made her feel like the last being left alive. The feeling was serene. The sky, the boat, the ocean, the planet: these things belonged to her now, and she to them, because there wasn't anything else. But occasionally an ink-splash in the distance would resolve itself into a sea-going bird powering towards the horizon, and Maddy would shout with pleasure as it flew over the mast. In her sleep she would hear the beat of wide wings, and, reminded of Feather, sleep soundly.

Time passed quite distinctly at first; then it began to liquefy. The day and date became insignificant – what mattered was light and weather. Some days the *Albatross* raced, and Maddy was too preoccupied to think; other days the boat plodded, and her mind was free to ramble. She liked to lie between the thwarts and let the swell rock her into daydreams. She thought about her childhood, her dolls and dollhouse. She thought about the convoluted quirks of life. It seemed remarkably peculiar that, just because she had once seen a young man on a beach, she was now bobbing in the middle of the ocean. "Life," she told the *Albatross*, "is full of caprice." Very cautiously, and very infrequently, she allowed herself to dwell on the fay. In another life she would be home, building a nest of twigs for the fay. A good tall tree would be needed, safe from marauders. Some birds plucked down from their own breasts to line their nests fluffily. The sun on Maddy's face felt very hot and fluid, like honey dripping from a fat hive. She cuddled up in her nest, the pointy shade of the leaves shuffling across her cheeks. She heard the snap of canvas and the sound of something burning. Soon she would need to climb higher, into the cradle of the tree, and find a leafy branch to shield the fay from the heat and the bees.

And then Maddy would sit up with a start and stare around at the water, remembering who she was. She blinked away visions of waterfalls and sandstone cities. This confusion of her mind made her afraid. Looking about with fresh eyes, the lunacy of her situation terrified her. She was alone, she was thirsty and worn, her skin was raw with sea-spray. She was floating nowhere, in the centre of nothing, with only the thin hull of a boat to keep her from sinking and disappearing, leaving nothing behind. She sat with her nails carved into the wood, and the indifferent ocean plashed in each direction for miles.

And then the cities would reappear on the skyline, and castles and lush woodlands as well, and Maddy would feel safe again, not lost at all, and gradually go back to sleep. She was dozing when a flying fish shot from the sea and landed, with a smacking sound, at the bottom of the boat. She yelped as the fish gasped and wriggled, flapping translucent wings. Recovering herself, she said, "Poor thing," and lifted the pale body, and dropped it over the side.

The flying fish squeaked, "Thank you," and disappeared.

Thereafter Maddy sat musing for a time, chewing her ragged thumbnail. A flying fish squeaking *thank you*.

Bad weather trundled in later that afternoon, and lumbered after the *Albatross* like a bear. Maddy pulled on her oilskin and slipped her feet into wellingtons. She rolled the drumming mainsail, secured the gaff and boom, and tied herself to the mast with a length of hawser rope. The gale hit the *Albatross* hard on the side, spun the craft in circles, yanked it into the air. Raindrops long as knitting needles speared from the sky. The ocean was thrilled by the havoc, and lurched anarchically. Maddy's sou'wester went overboard, as did her cooking pot. The sky was pitch, and gashed by lightning; loutish waves rose and slumped heavily as mudslides. At a moment when she was filled with desperation, Maddy opened her mouth and yelled for Feather. And half-expected him to appear, because she wanted him to so much.

When the tempest had passed, the water was fatigued, and the *Albatross* travelled on evenly. Maddy spent the evening wringing out her stockings and bailing the hull. Far off to port, a great striped marlin leaped, its nose a sapphire javelin. Water fanned behind it, the sunset iridescent on its flanks. It sliced back into the ocean like the sword of a knight.

The following day Maddy was dreamily admiring

a splendid onion-domed mosque that was floating as casually as an otter on the sea, and conducting a symphony being excellently played by an orchestra of pink-eyed, cat-faced musicians, when a green turtle bobbed its head from the waves and asked, "Have you seen a marlin around here?"

Maddy stopped conducting and peered overboard. "Actually, I have. I saw one yesterday."

"Ha!" The turtle barked in triumph. "I knew it! He thinks he can get away from me, but he won't! He *won't!*" With that, it scooped the water and dived. Maddy sat and stared, pouting, but it didn't reappear.

When next a shadow passed the boat, Maddy shouted, "Excuse me!"

The shadow belonged to a mako shark, which propped its steely head from the water and clashed, "Yes? What?"

It was disconcerting to speak to so many teeth. "I was wondering," Maddy fumbled, "if you know where Feather is? I need to ask him a question, you see."

"Don't know, don't care," said the mako, and vanished with a slash of fins. Stung by this rebuff, Maddy crawled underneath the thwarts to feel sorry for herself.

The next morning she saw a sunfish. Once, when she was small, Maddy had seen a sunfish caught in a trawler's net. The unfortunate beast, flat and round as a breakfast table, had attracted a crowd to the pier. It had had a sweet expression, Maddy remembered. "Excuse me?"

The sunfish glanced past its witch-hat dorsal fin. "May I help you?"

"Please, do you happen to know where Feather is? There's something I have to ask him."

The sunfish looked askance. "Know the name, but can't put a face. I never *can* put a face – can you? What you want is a dolphin. I don't like to speak spitefully, but dolphins always think they know everything."

"Thank you," said Maddy; and sat back to wait for a dolphin.

But in fact she saw nothing for many days, and several times started to cry. The sun was too hot, the ocean too cold, the boat was never still. She was surrounded by strangers, she was utterly lost, her quest was ridiculous and futile. She was famished, her skin itched, there was nothing interesting to do. Sleeping, she dreamed of her plush clean bed, a bath filled with bubbly water. At the very worst moments she ransacked her heart, searching the clutter for solace. Searching, mostly, for a remnant of Feather – the timbre of his voice, the scent of him. Drooping and weary, she wove her fingers between his, and leaned against his shoulder.

Suddenly the nose of the *Albatross* plunged, hurling Maddy from her seat. Beneath the boat frothed a rumpus like a battleship going down. It was a humpback whale, breaching and diving. "Excuse me!" Maddy bawled. "Sir, you'll sink us!"

The whale raised its enormous grey head, water sluicing from its smiling mouth and down the grooves of its throat. Its voice, when it spoke, was harmonious. "My apologies."

"Oh no, it was really my fault," said Maddy. "Whale, by any chance have you seen Feather? I urgently need to ask him something."

"Indeed I have seen your Feather," replied the whale. "It was, mind you, some time ago."

Maddy's heart somersaulted, she scrambled to the prow. "Did he say where he was going?"

"Regretfully he did not, no. And he was being blown about by Zephyrus, so he could be anywhere now."

"Zephyrus? Who is Zephyrus?"

"The west wind." The humpback rolled its tiny eye. "You might get some sense out of it, if you're lucky."

Maddy thanked the whale for its help, and sat back to consider. It is one thing to converse with aquatic life, but quite another to address a wind. Night was coming, and she lay down on the floor of the *Albatross*, a blanket folded under her head.

When she woke, the sky was very black, and a girl as airy as an owlfly's wing was perched on the bowsprit, gazing at her. The girl wore a gown that was tattered and dripping; her arms were matted with seaweed. Maddy could see the moon and a scattering of stars through her gauzy chest. She sat up and asked sharply, "Who are you?"

The girl smiled furtively, batting her lashes. Her voice was trill, and unpleasantly breathy. "Just a lost soul who went down with the ship," she said, as if she were ordering champagne. "There are so many of us, more than anyone can count. But we're all so bored with each other's company! We love to meet new people. This is a nice boat you have."

"Thank you," said Maddy. "Don't touch it."

"What are you doing out here by yourself? You're so far from home."

"I'm looking for someone," Maddy said. "I'm perfectly all right. Please don't worry about me."

The diaphanous girl pouted, and fiddled with her seaweed. "Come down and dance with us," she suggested. "We have a ten-piece band."

"Thank you but no," replied Maddy. "I'm looking for the west wind – do you know it?"

The apparition's eyes widened into sodden circles. "Zephyrus!" she shrilled. "It was Zephyrus who sank our ship! Stay away from Zephyrus! Be warned, be warned, be warned!"

"Oh, for goodness sake," Maddy sighed, and lit the lamp, which caused the phantom girl to frizzle up like a hair in a flame.

The *Albatross* sailed on, in endless pursuit of the horizon. Maddy wondered what would happen if she somehow reached that elusive line. She would topple over the edge of the world and come face to face with – what? A land where trees walked, and people

sprouted roots? Another girl, in another vessel, traversing an upside-down ocean? Is that what Feather had
been thinking about, as he stared at the horizon – a
place where everything was topsy-turvy? Maddy lay in
the bottom of the boat, warbling tunelessly to herself,
her thoughts riding the air like ribbons untied. She
lifted a hand and began to lazily trace her important
question onto the clouds. *How can you know...* Before
she could finish, the clouds coasted apart, and the
words plunked into the sea.

Her head was hanging over the side of the boat
when she saw a scrawny viperfish slunk up from the
deep. "What brings you here?" she asked.

The viperfish spoke through ludicrous teeth too
big for its head. Its voice was lean and long. "Battle
on. Kraken versus leviathan at dusk."

"You wouldn't happen to have seen Feather? I'm
looking for him. There's something he knows that I
want to know."

"I live at ocean's bottom," replied the viperfish
snarkily. "I don't get visitors."

"No need to be ungracious," Maddy said. "In that case, do you know where I'd find Zephyrus?"

"West wind? Probably be at battle. It likes argie-bargie."

Finally, something that sounded promising. "May I follow you there?"

"Aaaruggh!" screeched the fish. "Only if you don't dally! I can't stand waiting!"

So Maddy hoisted the sails and put the *Albatross* into a clip, sprinting in the wake of the lightning-fast fanged beast. Throughout the afternoon they raced towards the battle site. Maddy noticed other creatures streaming in from miles around – basking sharks, and schools of sockeye salmon; morays and herds of gigantic cuttlefish. Killer whales glided handsomely beneath the waves; auks dashed past in dozens. Leopard seals snapped their jaws as they flashed by the boat; stingrays wafted past like fainting spells. Maddy kept the *Albatross* tipped steep before the wind. White sharks and barracoutas sniped at the boat's silhouette; in the sky wheeled a flock of jet-winged frigate birds. Jellyfish undulated on the ocean's surface, trailing sparkling stingers. It was a rough and cutthroat crowd, and Maddy held tight to the tiller.

She felt the battle before she saw it. As the sun began to droop in the sky, the ocean grew choppy, and the *Albatross* bounced. Soon the prow was lunging skyward, then pointing straight down; water flooded across the floor, and thumped the stern bullishly. Looking along the bowsprit, Maddy saw the ocean was boiling. She pushed the anchor hastily over the side. As the bolt of metal disappeared into the dark she saw a vast pale spectre slip by: the white whale. It glanced at her without interest, the anchor spinning in the turbulence of its flukes.

Just then the water began to tear – Maddy clamped her arms around the mast. From the distant waves erupted a smoke-snorting monster, its brow bulky as a stagecoach, its chest a mountainside. It swung its armoured head and roared, shooting scarlet flames into the sky, crisping the wings of a spectating rukh, which shrieked like a harpy in fury. The ocean seethed as the sea-monster yawed about, its gaping mouth brandishing fortress-pike teeth. The leviathan was gargantuan and hideous, the most fearsome thing Maddy had ever seen. It stank of burning wood and rotting meat. Unexpectedly, the malevolent head was plastered by sinewy legs as thick as oaks and pied as death, which lashed from the water and suctioned to the monster's bulging jaws. The kraken held on mightily as the leviathan hauled it from the waves and flung the sleek body skyward, knives of water flinging everywhere. Round and around the two legendary creatures careered, the leviathan tangled in tentacles and bellowing, the kraken silent as a tomb, its huge eyes flatly reflecting the clouds and the sea. The ocean threw up cliffs of waves that crashed down in every direction. The giant squid beneath the *Albatross* changed colour with enthusiasm; the killer whales breached, pluming water into the air. In the sky a flock of crossbow jaegers dodged and screamed hoarsely. The leviathan's jaws slammed together and lopped off one of the kraken's tentacles, which fell into the ocean spurting fetid oil. The limb was instantly seized by a spangly serpent, which sped away jeeringly with its prize. The kraken seemed to feel no pain: it tightened its grip on the leviathan's head, buckling the monster's reptilian scales. The leviathan sucked down a cavernful of air, heaved it out as a torrent of flame. Maddy felt the heat punch past her, blocked her ears to its awful sound. The fire sheared over the water, sending a pod of walruses into woofing panic.

As the monsters warred and the sea animals hared about, the ocean began to spin. Loosely at first, the water looped the combatants as though it would fence them in; as the fighters raged on, the water spun faster; then faster and faster, and faster again, until it was flying like quicksilver and became not merely water but a whirlpool, which is water gone mad. Maddy watched in horror as the flashing hoop began to widen across the waves, its glassy centre sucking down towards the sea floor. The kraken and the leviathan, caught in the rotating maw, fought on ferociously, forced together by the water now, unable to break apart. Maddy dragged in the anchor and pinned the oars, aware she had just moments to escape the maelstrom's grip. Even as she splashed the blades into the foam, the kraken and the leviathan were snatched under the waves, the whirlpool effortlessly stronger than both of them. The ocean circled violently, the whirlpool scooping up and swallowing everything in its reach; every creature that was able to turned and frantically fled. Maddy pulled against the oars, and the *Albatross* lurched back – only to pitch forward immediately, charging for the whirling rings. Maddy wailed in terror, her heart banging in her ears. Her boat was captured, and so was she – there was no salvation in jumping overboard. In the next moment she would be sucked into the funnel of pounding water, where the *Albatross* would break apart and she would be spun into oblivion. She jerked the oars pathetically as the boat skipped towards the vortex, helpless as a kitten on a chain. Petrified, she had only one clear thought: that Feather had left her to fight alone. Feather didn't care what happened to her.

Then, inexplicably, the boat jumped backward, bucking like a pony. The sails sagged, puffed again, turned inside-out. Against all logic, the *Albatross* changed course, wrenching itself from the grip of the maelstrom, swinging to starboard, and speeding for clear water. Maddy clung dripping to the oars, speechless with astonishment. The breeze whipped up by the racing boat pulled her hair and billowed her oilskin. The boat rushed on until the whirlpool vanished in the distance, and the ocean lay smooth all around.

Then a voice said, "Hello! That was a close call! One more moment, and you would have been feeling rather dizzy! I hear you've been looking for me?"

"Zephyrus?" Maddy peeped.

"The one and only!" The west wind blew friskily, riffling the sails. "How may I be of assistance?"

"Zephyrus!" Galvanized by relief, Maddy jumped to her feet. "I'm looking for Feather. I need to ask him a question. A whale said you'd seen him."

"I certainly have! I helped *him* too. I am quite thoughtful like that."

Maddy clapped her hands to her cheeks. "Please," she beseeched the tangerine sky, "please, please, would you tell me where he is?"

"Please, please, please, where, where, where. Now let me *think*. Let me try to *remember*." The wind twanged the halyards and danced on the planks teasingly, hanging her on tenterhooks. Finally it volunteered, "Feather's on an Island of Stillness, not far from here."

"Oh! … An Island of Stillness? What's that?"

"Don't you know anything?" Zephyrus gusted smugly. "It's an *island* that is *still*. Whoever lives on an Island of Stillness is granted their dearest desire – forgetfulness, fulfilment, that kind of thing. They live that way forever, punished or unpunished, forgiven or unforgiven, remembering or forgetting, smart, stupid, happy, sad. The islands used to float about, following the summer, until somebody realized that the islands should stand still. Because that's what endless fulfilment is, isn't it? That's what forgetfulness is. Just stopping still. So the islands stopped floating, and now, on an Island of Stillness, everything is still."

"How awful that sounds," mused Maddy.

Zephyrus shrugged breezily. "You'd be surprised. Some people *like* things that way."

Maddy looked at the clouds. "Zephyrus," she said, "will you take me to him? So I can have an answer, finally?"

"Since you ask so nicely," the wind replied, "I suppose I will. I haven't got anything better to do. But remember, it's *Feather's* island, not yours. It's *his* dearest desire, not yours. His answer might not be what you want to hear. And anyway, does a girl who's voyaged across an ocean without compass or maps, who's talked to whales and wind and watched sea-monsters war, need an answer from anyone?"

Maddy hesitated, glancing away. Her eye was caught by her reflection wobbling beneath her. Gazing at her from the water was a girl who knew the friendship of narguns and trees. She'd weathered the bafflement of her childhood, and her bleak school years. She'd survived the disappearance of her travelling father, and the shattering loss of the fay. She'd poured the best of herself into love, and seen that love turned away; yet she'd managed to keep faith in herself. Was there any answer to any question that such a girl couldn't discover for herself?

"But you have come such a long way, haven't you?" prompted Zephyrus. "It would be a shame to give up. Every journey must be finished."

A little flame in Maddy's heart had simmered to almost nothing: now it sprang up again. "That's true." She smiled. "Every journey must be finished."

With that, the boat's nose swung to face a new direction. The sails filled, the rudder dipped, and with an electric, tiger-like leap, the *Albatross* began cutting through the water. Maddy sat at the tiller, her hands on her knees, watching the ocean flash by. Overhead, the sky was mottling cobalt and ruby. The earliest stars came out to glitter on the waves. The moon hung frostily, close to the water, a skating rink for fireflies.

Darkness had not closed in completely for the night, but the sky was stained a rich navy when the sails began to flutter, the boat slowed down, and a low, rocky island rose into view. "Land ahoy," said Zephyrus, and Maddy stepped to the prow, her blood hammering.

Every atom in Maddy fizzed with nervousness by the time the *Albatross* beached on the island's shore. She was tempted to beg the west wind to take her straight home. The sand made a raspy grinding noise against the boat's wooden keel: to Maddy, it was the sound of resistance, a sound that said *begone*. Zephyrus was no comfort at all. "Good luck!" the west wind chortled. "Better you than me! Whistle when you want me to get you out of here."

Maddy watched the wind sweep away, a dust-devil of sand blustering in its wake. She hoped

153

it wouldn't go far. Never in her life – not in the pine forest at home after Feather had gone, not in the juddery midst of the cold ocean – had she felt as isolated and apprehensive as she did now. For the first time in such a long time, Maddy was close to Feather – but she felt high up and untouchable, lost to everywhere.

She lit the lamp and carried it with her up the beach. She had imagined the sand would be clean and powdery, but it was coarse under her bare feet. She turned up the flame and held the lamp aloft, expecting to see palm trees and pools of azure water and the tumbling quills of gorgeous birds. Instead she saw craggy ochre rocks piled haphazardly upon one another, a harsh rent scenery like the floor of an exhausted quarry. She picked a path over and between the boulders, slipping on yellow grit. As she climbed, she listened for the grumble of hyenas or rattlesnakes. The island seemed the sort of place such bad-tempered creatures might call home.

She struggled to the point of a jagged peak, hoping that beyond the citadel of rocks might sprawl a lush oasis. At a height, the breeze blew sulkily cool. The indigo sky and burnished moon cast a velvet light over the island, which was small – Maddy could see, not too far away, the ocean looping the land's other side. Looking down from her vantage point she was pleased to discover clusters of palm trees, their spiky fronds lounging from skinny, flaking trunks. But there weren't many trees, and they stood apart like strangers, and around their feet was worn, bristly ground. They were also very quiet trees, making not the faintest rustle – as if they had spied, and disliked, and agreed to be frosty towards her. Between her lookout and the island's opposite shore Maddy saw no streams of water, no swaying grass, no flowers or mounds of rich soil. There was nothing that moved; there was a pallor of strange deadness; there was nothing pleasing to see.

"Feather!" Maddy yelled, and not even a skink took fright. She stared about herself, thinking that obviously the west wind had made a mistake. Feather, who loved the pulse of living things, could never have desired to find himself in this barren place.

But then a sure voice said, "Maddy," and she turned, and he was there.

In the moonlight, he looked more beautiful than ever – more feathery, more silvery, more smoky and unplaceable. Scraps of cloth hung about him like the plumes of a ruffled bird. His fair hair was longer, and disarrayed again, draping into his eyes. He looked strong and lean and stood lightly, coppery around the edges. Maddy had always imagined herself running to him, leaping into his arms, both of them laughing exultantly. Instead she hung back, warm with shyness, and the air enclosing them was still. "Hello, Feather," she said.

He said, "Come and sit under the trees."

She followed him down the cliffs to the flat sandy land below. After all the months of talking to him in her head, Maddy was bewildered to find she had nothing to say. Her mind was empty of inspiration, her mouth hollow of words. The importance had completely sputtered out of the question she'd burned for so long to ask him. She felt as brutish as the cliff boulders. Feather, walking ahead, glanced over his shoulder at her. "I wish you could see the island in daylight," he said, and his voice was the same, as restful as swans. "The rocks gleam like chests filled with jewels. The grass is green as a river bank. Sleeping on the earth in the afternoon is like sleeping on a waterlily in the middle of a lake."

Maddy glanced down at the crusty dry dirt – it didn't feel like a lake to her, but rough as a lion's tongue. Shrivelled grass, husky as hay, cracked under each step. The rocks were pocked and charmless, inert angular things. She could even smell the burly odour of decaying seaweed. Surely mere daylight couldn't make a difference to this. "Is light bewitching here?" she asked, suddenly thinking she'd found the explanation. "Does sunrise transform everything into something lovely?"

Feather shook his head. "No, it's not bewitching light. Everything is always lovely. In the moonlight, it's lovely. In the daylight it's lovelier, that's all."

"Oh," said Maddy; and felt prickly with awkwardness, and let the subject drop.

They stopped in the centre of a ring of palms; Maddy sat down to pick burrs from her feet while Feather built a fire of grass and sticks. The sky had thickened to an incubus-blue but the moon was low and lustrous, brighter than the lamp. Mosquitoes and tiny midges arrived to fumble about peskily. Feather did not seem to notice them. He sat down and looked through the flames at her, fire glinting off his eyes. "It's nice to see you," he said.

His voice was so familiar and evocative to Maddy,

such an unpredicted cause of pain: hearing it made her remember everything, and forget the brave girl she'd seen reflected in the sea. The sorrows that had bleached her life returned, spilling like chilled water down her spine. Her heart gave an oceanic lurch: the fay was gone, her great love was gone, there was nothing worth waking for. *Come back*, she ached to say, *come to me.* "I've missed you," she said.

Feather looked aside. "See the spider webs on the leaves." He pointed. "A galaxy is caught inside them."

Maddy turned her head reluctantly, saw two or three stars hanging like parched bugs inside webs, a sight that seemed somehow annoying to her. Indeed, anything her eye glanced upon managed to vaguely irritate her. She looked back at Feather, asked, "Is this island the thing you were longing for, all those days and nights when you roamed the beach so restlessly?"

"Of course," he said, as if she were a child asking the most quaintly naive question in the world.

Maddy looked at him over the weaving flames – at his slender brown feet, his square empty hands, the scaffold of bones in his shoulders. She couldn't think of a thing to reply. Seeing him should have been thrilling, but instead she felt shut behind a wall. The island was horrible, all her struggle seemed wasted, and Feather was someone she couldn't understand. *Come back*, she might have pleaded: *Return, be what you were.* Rather she said, "Zephyrus says that an Island of Stillness grants a person's dearest desire. Will you tell me what your island has given you, Feather?"

Feather replied, "Eternal peace."

He said it simply, as he'd say the name of a dog or plant, as though eternal peace was an everyday thing you might trip over if you didn't watch where you walked – but proudly too, it plainly being something he considered enviable. Maddy cocked her head, frowning. "Is that why you left?" she asked. "Because I didn't bring you peace? I loved you, we trusted one another, I would never have hurt you, we were friends: wasn't there peace in that?"

Feather sighed, and shifted his place, because he heard plaintiveness in her voice, and plaintiveness can be a bore. He poked the fire with a stick and raised a wraith of hot sparks, looking away from her. "Sometimes," he said, "love is not the strongest or the most important thing in the world. For you to be happy, Maddy, you need someone different to what I am. For you to be happy, I would have had to change. And I did change – all that I could. But I must be true to myself, as you're always true to yourself. And I'm true to myself when I'm here."

Maddy smiled thinly. Without doubt, she had always loved him more than he'd loved her. His love had been mediocre: her love had been a hawk. She would willingly have changed herself for him, eternally, utterly – he'd needed only to ask. The imbalance between them was painful, and made her want to cause pain. "But what exactly *are* you, when you're here?" she asked. "With me, you were vital, and wanted, and adored. What are you, what use are you, what *good* are you, in this lonesome place? Eternal peace might make you peaceful, Feather, but that's *all* it will make you. You'll never be anything else."

She clamped her mouth shut, her words flying off like bats – her voice was probably the loudest thing the island had ever heard. Feather gazed steadfastly into the fire. "If you can't understand it, Maddy," he said, "then I can't explain it to you. Sometimes you must do what is right for your blood, your heart – for your spirit. Maybe this place isn't perfect, but I'm supposed to be here – here, alone – and this is where I will stay."

Maddy said nothing. Her nails were dug in her palms. She glanced away into the darkness, where there was nothing she wanted to see. How curious it was, that this person she craved so much should crave something so different to her. A small voice inside her was piping, *Come back! Come back! Come back!* But she let it cry unheeded, turned her face from it. The palm leaves rustled, the fire popped, the ocean slushed the shore. Maddy thought she must not have a spirit – or that, if she did, it was a boorish thing. Her spirit knew no shades of grey, only black and white. Grief and happiness, loss and gain. "Well," she said eventually, looking back at him, "are you happy now, Feather?" And she hoped, more than she'd ever hoped for anything, that he would say he was. What purpose was there in all that had happened, if both of them must still suffer?

His silver eyes lifted to her; he said, "My nature is comforted here."

Maddy nodded. She felt abruptly tired, and ready to go home; she hankered to be aboard the *Albatross*, roving the vast free sea. She could hardly bear how alienated she felt, here on this island of Feather's dearest desire: if she were forced to stay, Maddy would stalk the beach just as Feather had done, relentlessly scanning the horizon for elsewhere. And it was dismal talking to this being who looked like Feather, and spoke like him, who was even tinged with the wheatfield smell of him – but was just an echo of the Feather she'd loved, the one she'd longed to see again. Those days were finished, that Feather was gone, the only place he lived now was in the past. And she resented this new Feather spoiling her memories of the old, which were the most cherished things that she owned. "I'm glad you've found peace, Feather," she said. "I'm pleased you were able to forget me. Because how else could you live with the hurt you caused? It's a terrible thing, to love, and be left behind."

"I believe you," he said softly – and looking up she saw a spangle of someone she had known. "I haven't forgotten you, Maddy. Part of me never stops remembering you. Remembering you comforts my nature now, too."

She watched him shimmer, turn smoky and flare with light. Somewhere inside him her Feather survived, holding her hand in his own. The realization stung her, and made her eyes smart: she did not know if his absence would be less painful now, or much, much worse. But this was the Feather she had searched for, the one who would most understand. Hastily, before he vanished, she said, "I need to ask you a question, Feather. It's a question bigger than the world. By the time I guessed you knew the answer, you were already gone. But I need the answer so badly that I crossed the horizon to find you."

"And I'm here," said Feather. "So ask."

Maddy drew a breath, rehearsed the words in her head, and asked, "How can you know love, and lose it, and go on living without it, and not feel the loss forever?"

"You can't," Feather answered. "You feel the loss forever. But you put it in a safe corner of yourself, and bit by bit some of your sorrow changes into joy. And that's how you go on living."

Maddy saw it in her mind, a great coin flipping slowly, showing first the whiplash tail of sadness, next the warm facet of joy. Sorrow and joy, bonded so closely that occasionally they spun inside each other. "And you take pride in knowing you're capable of great love," she said, "and live in the knowledge that you can feel it again."

"…Yes," said Feather. "You can feel it again."

After that, there seemed little else to say. They sat in easy companionship for a while, feeding sticks into the fire and reminiscing about the cottage and the beach. They did not talk of the fay or the pond, or about his leaving in the middle of the night, because these were things that had not yet been safely cornered somewhere. Their conversation was suffused with a poignancy, which they pretended didn't exist. They talked like two old soldiers with not much in common once the battlefield stories were done.

When the moon hung directly over their heads, Maddy knew it was time to go. She shook the dust from her oilskin and scratched her mosquito bites. Feather walked with her down to the sand, to where the *Albatross* was aground. They stood side-by-side at the boat's pointy prow, reaching for the right things to say, hoping to make these last moments soar, but flailing like drenched birds. "Will you be all right?" Maddy asked, because it was important that he be so. It would never make her happy to think of him as sad.

He shrugged, smiling sweetly. "Of course. Will you?"

"Of course," she said too.

"And do you really like my island?" he asked.

Maddy looked up at the ugly garrison of rocks, smelt the cloyed, seaweedy air, felt the sand gravelly between her toes. Eternal peace was an awe-inspiring thing: but it was also a frightening and stultifying thing. Here on his Island of Stillness, Feather would never feel frustration, anticipation, regret, or glee. He'd be immune to confusion, impatience, disappointment, and surprise. He would not yell with exhilaration, he would know no fear. He would not be irate, he would never weep. He would be stone, unmalleable, living a stone's life, as bland as the Island of Stillness itself. Despite this, she said, "It's beautiful, Feather," and it was, if it made him happy.

They pushed the *Albatross* into the water, and Maddy climbed aboard. As the waves pulled the boat out to sea, Maddy watched Feather become smaller and smaller. Finally, when he was just a tiny speck that could hardly be seen in the dark, she whistled for the west wind. Zephyrus put a shoulder to the canvas and sped her lightly away. When she next looked back, Maddy could see only the thick night sky and the thicker blackness of the ocean below it. The Island of Stillness, she knew, was standing where it had come to a halt centuries ago: it was she who was gone.

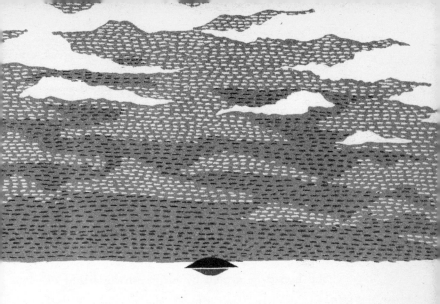

Maddy had plenty of time to think during the long voyage home. The west wind steered the *Albatross* while she sat on the seat with her chin in her hands, turning over matters in her mind. She thought about Feather shrinking smaller and smaller as she sailed away. By the time the conifer forest that surrounded her cottage appeared as olive stubble in the distance, Feather would be tinier than a grain of sand, tinier than the tiniest speck of dust that might catch in the eye of the most miniature insect ever known. He filled her heart hugely though, so there was hardly room for anything more. In her memory he flew as wide-winged as an eagle. She wondered if his shadow would hover over her forever, a bruise in the background of the rest of her life, a wound that pained when it was deliberately or accidentally knocked. Strangely, she wanted it to be this way. If the hurt of Feather healed, metamorphed into joy, she might one day forget him. And she did not want to forget him.

She hoped he would be happy on his Island of Stillness. She wondered if he would ever think of her wistfully, spoiling his serenity.

She would never see Feather again, Maddy knew. That part of her life was over. And the best she could do was take what she'd known – of Feather, of the fay, of the future she'd imagined in the forest's shade – and salvage something from it. She had lost, but loss has its own quality and promise. She could gather up the bare bones of her life and build from them something wiser and more intricate than what she'd had before.

"Thank you," she said to Zephyrus, when the *Albatross* glided into the bay.

"My pleasure," said the wind. "Any time. I like you, you know. You remind me of me, and I *really* like me. You don't want peace or sameness. You know that life is for going, not stopping."

Maddy asked, "Do I?"

The wind said, "You *do*. But when life goes, it goes fast, Maddy: so be careful. Don't waste your time wanting what you can't have."

"From now on," Maddy promised, "I will try."

She let down the sails, tied the boat to the pier, slipped off her oilskin, and walked home.

The west wind was right: life lasts a long time, but it goes by in a blink. There are plenty of quiet hours in which to sit and think, yet so little time to make decisions and get the serious things done. As soon as she opened the door of the cottage, Maddy knew that living within a dark forest wasn't something she should do. She was not, after all, Snow White. She packed her favourite things into a box, and tied down the lid. The nargun was crammed in a corner of the room, its black face full of worry. "I don't need your protection any more," she told it. "I must look after myself now. But I hope that you will always be my friend." The beast pranced to its feet and wagged its stumpy tail like a pup. When Maddy finished packing, she left the cottage for the last time, closing the door behind her. She glanced back several times as she walked, her heart panging and protesting. But soon there was nothing to see except pine trees, and she turned her face to the front.

"Good riddance to bad rubbish," was Mama's verdict of Feather. She swallowed a mouthful of wine. "I told you he was intolerable, Matilda. Hopefully one day everyone will forget this sorry saga, and you can hook a widower."

Maddy's father, slicing roast lamb, said, "He was never good enough for you."

And although everything had been so futile and disappointing, Maddy said, "I've never known anyone better than Feather."

Mama gave a snort. "I wonder if he speaks so highly of you, while he's lazing around wasting his life and making mayhem of yours. How can you care a fig for someone who casts you aside – in favour of what?"

"Of truth." The word occurred to Maddy from nowhere, crisp as crystal. "I'm glad I know somebody who would choose honesty over everything."

"My goodness! How whimsical! Truth! What is that?"

Maddy shuddered. She would not speak of Feather

at this table. She looked to her father and said, "Papa, I don't want to sit about doing nothing. I have been thinking: I want to go to the war."

"What?" The boy stretched out on the settee sat up on his elbows. "War? What war?"

Matilda leaned back in her chair. "Surely, at school, you've learned about the war."

"Of *course*." His eyes thinned, he resented being suspected ignorant. "But what was the war doing in *your* poky town? The shooting and trenches were on the other side of the world. How did they get to *your* dinner table?"

"Even *our* poky little town had newspapers," Matilda explained. "My father had them delivered to the house every day. I read them, and I was amazed. While I'd been gone, such a foolish thing had happened. Someone had fired a gun and killed an heir to a throne, and all the countries surrounding the street corner where the heir died had used his death as a reason to pounce into war – as if war is a child's game played with sticks and stones, and its hurts can be healed with a kiss. But this wasn't a game at all. Every day the papers printed lists of men who were maimed, missing, dead; and the lists grew longer, and never seemed to stop growing."

"So did you want to become a soldier, and help win the war?" The boy smiled at the idea.

"Not exactly," Matilda replied. "I was brave, but not *that* brave. Besides, the men who were so wantonly slaughtering one another were still gentlemen enough to believe that a battlefield was not a nice place for a lady... But the women in those fighting countries were helping in other ways. With the men gone, it was they who were driving the trucks, running the factories, harvesting the fields. It was they who were manufacturing the ammunition. And they were caring for the soldiers who were sent home broken, unable to play that awful game any more."

The boy nodded, and lay down again, his hands folded under his head.

"I told Papa I wished to go where I'd be useful." Matilda closed her eyes and saw the dining table, the candlelight, the roast lamb and jug of mint sauce, the expression on her father's face. "I knew I could do something more important with my life than paint watercolours and attend the theatre and shop for buttons and bows to match a new dress."

And she had wanted to crowd her hours with noise and busyness and a thousand thoughts that were not sunk nose-deep in the past. "That was a good idea," said the boy.

"That, perhaps, is a good idea." Mama licked a scarlet drop from her chin. "The first good idea you've had in a long time. Send you away. Give everyone time to forgive you."

Papa sighed, and the look on his face was sad but accepting, because he understood that his daughter needed this thing.

So within a few weeks Maddy was aboard ship once more, sailing, this time, for a certain destination, on a boat which had an engine, and thus no need for wind. But Maddy, standing on the deck, spread her hands to Zephyrus, and let him rush through her fingers. She stood at the railing and searched the horizon, but from the deck of a big metal ship such things as spellbound islands are frivolous, and never exist.

She found a place where she could be useful in a grand stone house circled by a park of elm trees and grass, a place where soldiers who'd been injured in the war were sent to learn the laws of their new legless or armless lives. Maddy washed the men, and wrote their letters; read to them, and wheeled them around the grounds in chairs. She spooned supper to their lips and wiped their stained, scarred cheeks. She held their hands when they woke at night, soaked and shouting with nightmares; when fever made them call for their mothers it was Maddy who dabbed their faces and cooed them back to sleep. She wore a white dress, learned to roll cigarettes, went whole nights without sleeping, slept on a cot; and let clouds move over her past.

It was a new world inside the grand house, more indomitable and more traumatic than any world Maddy had known. She saw men struggling to surface from drowning despair; men who, suffering dreadfully, nevertheless managed to laugh. These men had lost much, but had somehow kept their humour, their goodness, their trust. They had not let anyone take from them these things that were most worth keeping. They made Maddy, sometimes, ashamed of herself.

Soldiers often arrived at the house with their heads balled in bandages, having been blinded by poisonous gas. Something about these patients kept Maddy awake at night. It troubled her to think they would never see stags or cathedrals again. They would never see rain falling, or rivers, or woodland meadows or shooting stars, things that are meant for everyone to see. They would never see the faces they'd loved to see – their sweethearts, their children, their dogs. These men had lost something bigger than an arm or a leg: they had lost sight of beautiful things. Maddy covered her eyes and imagined her life without the images collected inside her head: and the vacuum of blackness she saw there made her gasp.

At the end of the war, Maddy wrote to her father announcing that she wanted to be a doctor. Eyes and eyesight, she'd discovered, interested her. Maybe, if she learned enough about sight, she could give it back to blind men.

Her father, receiving this letter, rolled his own eyes to the ceiling. The iron man would have preferred that his dreamy daughter and wayward child come home to occupy herself with nothing more challenging than trying on pearls. But her other father, the one who had once given Maddy a mirror, wanted her to be happy. So he called upon his influential friends and made donations where they counted, and Maddy enrolled at university to learn about skeletons and senses and germs. She learned how people live, and why they die; she learned about infection and cancer, tuberculosis and haemorrhage, and the body's armies of cells. She cut open dead people, and sewed them back together; she stared into bottles of pieces and parts. She learned how babies are formed and born and raised; she learned the many ills of the old. She ignored the teasing of her fellow students, who thought doctoring was best left to boys. When they badgered her with questions, intrigued by her aloofness, she told them nothing about herself, and eventually they let her be. Maddy did not want friends or adversaries, let alone a beau. She wanted to understand eyes. She sat with her books in her chambers at night, making notes and concentrating until her own eyes grew blurry and she sagged in her chair. Nothing was easy, and sometimes she failed, and sometimes she thought that the fairy stories were right, that there must indeed be easier ways of living happily ever after; but defeat is a poor ending to any tale, so she kept trying. When the wind rumpled her papers and the pages of her books, Maddy would smile and murmur tolerantly, "Yes, Zephyrus, I know."

Sometimes, when things were difficult, she thought about Feather. It rested her to think of him.

She saw him standing in the breeze, the wind ransacking his hair. She saw birds wheeling in squally circles over his head. She wondered what he was doing at that moment – sleeping maybe, or swimming. She'd look away from her work, as if she might glimpse him, but see just a window, a wall.

Her father died suddenly, not long after a brass plate bearing Maddy's name was screwed to the door of her white-walled surgery. She read the black-edged telegram and wept so fiercely she thought she would crinkle like a leaf and blow away. For weeks she dreamed of Papa, a tall broad man scaling pyramids and the Eiffel Tower. "Look up, Maddy, look up!" he called, as he climbed higher and higher. His loss reminded her of other things. Years had passed, but she thought of the fay – no longer tiny, but older, and running, a plucky mischievous creature with unruly hair. She kicked a chair helplessly, and hurt her foot. *Where there's life there is loss.* Had Feather said that? His words in her memory were imperfect. *Take pride in knowing you're capable of love.*

In the beginning, the blind ex-soldiers were reluctant to be treated by her. There was still something barbarous and odd about Maddy; and she was youthful, and not stern, and she wasn't a man – in short, she was nothing a doctor should be. At first, only the poorest and most hopeless let her shine her torch into their eyes. Yet word soon spread that Maddy was a good doctor, because she didn't tell her patients to accept their blindness manfully, but let them howl and curse over the damage done to them. She understood that grief can live on long after it's ceased to be spoken of, and she encouraged her patients to speak to her. Gradually her waiting room became full – not just with ex-soldiers, but with infants born eyeless, and children who'd played with crackers, and elderly people whose vision was failing. She peered into grey eyes, hazel eyes, green and blue eyes, and eyes the same midnight colour as her own. Looking into pupils, Maddy pretended she could see everything her patient had seen, and might one day see again. She operated, stitched, unwrapped bandages, let in light; she experimented with potions and pills. Often, however, she admitted defeat, and told her patients to look around while they could. Her young patients raved against their fates, the older ones accepted theirs with grace. The old people were coming to the end of their lives, and they sometimes talked about dying. When they wondered if there was a Heaven, Maddy said she supposed there could be. So many fabulous things existed – krakens and waterfalls, the sunny smell of wheat – why shouldn't there be a Heaven as well?

By the time she was a middle-aged woman, Maddy was quietly famous in her field, respected for her innovations and expertise. Every few years she embarked on a sea journey. Sometimes she voyaged with friends or colleagues; mostly she set out with no company except the ghost of her father. She travelled to relax; she travelled to refresh her cache of the world's most beautiful things. Cruising oceans, she looked through portholes for a glimpse of an Island of Stillness. She didn't expect to see one, of course, and she never did; it was just something to do to pass the time. It was hard for her to picture Feather's face now, and impossible to hear his voice. But whenever she happened to think of him, Maddy still felt a swirl in her heart. And although so much had faded from her memory, she knew that if she saw him, she would remember. She would remember his voice as if she had never stopped listening to it.

And when she thought of Feather, she thought of the fay – tall now, and occasionally rebellious, headstrong and casually kind. She would close her book and turn off the lamp and curl up under her blankets, and call herself a silly fool, and listen to the night.

Maddy's mother lived to become a crabby old woman. Her day-nurse found her one morning propped on her pillows, glaring at a ladies magazine, cold as yesterday's dinner. Maddy didn't weep fiercely at the news of her mother's death, feeling only a sense of regret for what might have been. She did not understand why Mama hadn't been happy with what life had given her, and knew she would have departed this world with a sniff of disgust. But she hoped there really was a Heaven where Mama could go, some exclusive resort where wealthy ladies found plenty of faults about which to satisfyingly complain.

After her mother died, the big seaside house in which Maddy had been born stood empty, and had to be sold. Maddy came home for the first time in untold years. It was eerie and enchanting to be returned after so long. Everything was altered, but still smelt the same – the wide rooms of the house, the eucalypt bushland, the cove with its rocky beach. Maddy was no longer young, and it took her many painstaking and tiring weeks to deal with the furniture and artworks and chinaware. In the attic, opening case after case, she felt herself travelling through time. A part of her hoped she would find the felt giraffe she'd forsaken as a child, but she didn't. But she did discover a box full of knick-knacks that had once decorated a cottage in a forest.

As she untied the cord that bound the box, Maddy was holding her breath. As she folded back the lid, she sniffed pine cones and pond water, muddy boots and a vegetable garden. Rummaging inside the box, she found a brass kaleidoscope, and a sepia photograph of a girl at the helm of a boat. For a moment, gazing at these relics, everything was keenly real, and happened only yesterday.

She tied up the box and set it aside with the keep-sakes she would send home; all else was auctioned, and the proceeds donated to Mama's foundling mites. The house by the ocean – the finest house in town – was sold and signed over to a new family. As Maddy walked down the carriageway for the final time, she realized she was no one's daughter now. She stopped calling herself Maddy, and turned into Matilda.

She had booked a cabin on a ship, meaning to sail away. But the day came to leave, and she didn't leave: instead she found a sweet-natured house in the suburbs, and decided to stay. Matilda was nearly old now, but like a child she'd become filled with a yearning for home. She had seen as much of the world as she needed to, and given sight wherever she could. When she could not give sight, she'd tried to give mettle: *change your sorrow into joy.* Now she wanted to be where she felt she belonged, where her father had walked, where a nargun had guarded her, where her life had been untame and secure.

In the years that followed, Matilda made some friends; the mellow shuffle of time softened her, so she became talkative and genial. Her house was filled with interesting objects, and she always ate fresh food. Each morning she did the crossword before setting out on a brisk walk. She drank a glass of wine in the evening for the sake of her blood, and visited her dentist once a year. She threw scraps into the garden for the birds, and always stopped to pat a dog. When television was invented, she went out and bought a set. She took photography lessons and painting lessons, and gave to charities; she read books about biology and well-lived lives. She pottered in her garden, planting bulbs and sweeping and turning a blind eye to the weeds. She needed stronger glasses, and tablets for her arthritic knuckles. Now and then she was absent-minded, which she never used to be. She would find herself leaning against the broom, drowsy with daydreams. Things she assumed she'd forgotten began returning to Matilda clearly. She recollected feelings, scents, colours and sounds – dancing in gilt palaces, yawning in fuggy libraries, diving in a white drift of snow. The heave of the ocean under her feet, the brashness of salt in the air. In the corner of her eye, a marlin leapt from the waves.

Leaning on her broom, Matilda remembered sailing away on the *Albatross*, leaving Feather marooned by peace. Although she was proud to have known him, there had been times, when she was younger, when she'd wished she never had. She had despised the sadness that hung inside her like old lace. It had taken such a long time to alchemize her grief into acceptance and forgiveness, gratitude and finally joy. But she had never doubted for an instant that she was lucky to have felt such love.

Matilda was standing on the mountain top, and looking back along the path she'd walked she was satisfied with what she saw. Her life had never been mystifying, as she'd once girlishly wished it to be: it had been, in its way, quite ordered and clear. There were things missing from it that she'd expected to have – things other people secured easily, but which she had been left without. Yet she believed she had lived a fulfilling life, a worthwhile life, a brave one. She had tried to be the person her father hoped she could be. Her heart was no longer a prison, but something without walls or a key. When Matilda thought of Feather now, which she almost never did, it was with soft affection and admiration for him, and a wisp of pity.

Matilda's eyes were so heavy she could hardly keep them open. She had a recollection of deciding to make dinner, though she wasn't particularly hungry; she fancied she could even recall chopping broccoli and stirring a pot. But there was no plate on the table before her, and no taste in her mouth. She wondered muzzily if she was remembering something done another day.

The boy was sitting up straight on the settee, and he appeared to be waiting for her.

"And now you're here." Her voice sounded

mumbly, she hoped she was making sense. She seemed to have grown inexplicably more feeble in an afternoon. Here she was, half-asleep, and it wasn't even dark outside.

The boy smiled, his grey eyes curving into crescents. Although he was waiting, he didn't seem impatient – he was not a foreboding guest at all. "You were pretty when you were young," he said, surprisingly. "Why didn't you ever find somebody else to like?"

Matilda's hands made a church steeple. "Oh, I liked. Some of the soldiers I met at the grand house during the war – some of the doctors and scientists I knew in later years – they were clever, funny, generous, good men. One or two of them I liked very much indeed. But it was never such love that made both of us want to stop searching for love."

"Huh." The boy said uncomfortably, "I wish it had been."

"Thank you," said Matilda. "Sometimes I did, too. But life is not a story, and things don't always turn out as you'd prefer. That doesn't mean you have failed, though."

"Hmm." The boy looked unhurriedly around the room. "But you're happy," he stated. "You've been happy with your life."

Matilda weighed her reply. "I'm happy to have been alive. I'm happy to have had the chance."

He looked at her. "If I ask a question, will you answer it?"

"Of course, if I can."

"All right." He shifted his slight frame. "Which did you need more: Feather, or the fay?"

It was something she had thought about before. "The sky needs the moon and the sun equally," she said. "Everyone needs food, but water as well. I needed Feather to keep me warm; the fay is the one I would have kept warm."

"I understand," said the boy.

Matilda sighed and smiled, knowing something was ended. She felt very welcoming towards her guest, though he had arrived so unexpectedly, on a day when she had given scant contemplation to anything beyond the weather and supper. She knew that part of her must have always been waiting for him – waiting forever, for years. "You're not as old as you should be," she observed.

He said, "I am the age you most often imagine me."

This was true. She'd imagined him as a tiny, pale-faced infant, and then as a slender boy. She'd imagined him as he would have been by now – very grown up, a proper man, maybe a doctor like herself, with tall children of his own. She would be a grandmother, a whole other person to the one she was now, somebody with photographs cluttering her mantel, the focus of loud attention at Christmas time.

But most often she had imagined him the way he looked this evening, sitting lightly on the settee: a fair-haired child of eleven or twelve, someone old enough to hold a serious conversation, too old to hold her hand – but young enough to want to be with her, young enough to play. He wore clothes of the type she'd have chosen for him, good strong boots, hardy red shirt, trousers that would last. He would have a coat, too, and she wished he would wear it more often. She had given him, over the years, so many Christian names, each dependent on her mood. There was no single word that seemed to permanently suit the delight that filled her on the day she had stood by a window and felt the shiver that was him.

She thought about all the years she'd been without him, and said, "It is lovely to see you."

All this talk of love abruptly became too much: the boy rolled his eyes in the manner of his grandfather, the iron man, and his mouth twisted down, an unravelling bow that Mama would have recognized. Matilda longed to hug him to her and squeeze him, feel the slimness of his bones and the featheriness of his hair and the warmth of his breath as he protested. The boy wore a cautious, amused expression, as if he knew exactly what she was thinking. But she stayed in her chair and kept her hands to herself, not wanting to torment him. "What happens now?" she asked.

"I think you just stand up, and walk away."

"I don't feel any pain," she remarked.

The boy shrugged. "I think that sometimes there's just sleep."

Matilda knew he was right. As a doctor, she had witnessed all sorts of dying. She had seen long and tiring struggles, conflicts waged like whirlwinds; and she'd seen dying that came quietly as a moth into the room, on soft dun fluttery wings. She wondered what had failed her – her heart, or her mind. Both of them, she had to admit, were in need of a rest. "Will you come with me?" she asked the boy, hopingly. She did not think she could bear to lose sight of him again.

"Yes." He nodded loosely. "I'll come."

Matilda looked around the lounge room for a final time, saying silent farewell to the objects that had decorated her life. Though she'd tried to do otherwise, she had never been able to stop cluttering her present with her past. Now somebody she didn't know would pack her treasures into plastic bags and carry them away. A life, at its end, is a pile of cloth and paper, and goods that can be bagged and labelled. None of the best things – the voice and the laugh, the tilt of the head, the things seen and felt and spoken – are allowed to stay behind.

Gazing about, Matilda remembered Peake, who was asleep on his mat. "What about my dog?" she asked, immediately alarmed. There is kindness in having the courage to say goodbye, but she could not leave her dog. There was no one who would care for him, no one who loved him much. The boy, however, answered calmly, "Peake can come. This is such a stuffy room – there's no fresh air in here. That heater is puffing out bad fumes. They make you too lazy to breathe, or stand, or let a dog out to chase cats. So Peake had better come too."

And Matilda realized it then, the dull slumberousness that was oozing past the heater's flames, as dangerous and overlookable as a snake coiled under a couch. She had lived her life alongside the elements – rock, earth, water, fire. The air that had filled her sails and kept her alive was now draining her strength and shutting her eyes. "Poor Peake," she whispered. "I'm sorry for being so careless. I should have called a plumber."

The boy said consolingly, "It will be nice to have Peake with us."

They looked at each other, and smiled with the nervous excitement of travellers beginning a journey. When she stood, Matilda was pleased to find that her limbs were weightless and her joints didn't ache. She looked down at the old lady who slumped in the chair, seeming nothing more unusual than asleep. On her face were the remnants of a smile. She had witnessed the world's most beautiful things, and allowed herself to grow old and unlovely. She had felt the heat of a leviathan's roar, and the warmth within a cat's paw. She had conversed with the wind and had wiped soldiers' tears. She had made people see, she'd seen herself in the sea. Butterflies had landed on her wrists, she had planted trees. She had loved, and let love go. So she smiled.

Matilda turned to the boy, who stood by the door. "Is it peaceful, where we are going?"

She held her breath waiting for his answer.

The boy said, "Only if you want it to be."

Beyond the door, very oddly, was an emerald ocean and a blue sky. A wooden boat bobbed on the water, and Matilda and the boy stepped into it. Matilda looked back to the little dog who lingered behind, uncertain if he had been invited. "Come on, Peake," she said, and he ran to her, springing into the boat. The boy hauled up the anchor and Matilda hoisted the sails; the slim boat caught the billowing breeze, jumped the ripples of frothy green waves, and was away.

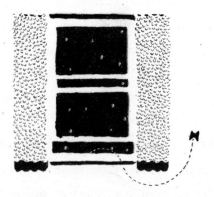